The Vengeful Parent

Shane Reed

Copyright

Chapter 1

The hollow echo of Ava Jennings' footsteps reverberated through the empty hallway of Pine View Elementary, each step a haunting reminder of the solitude that surrounded her. The weight of the box in her arms seemed to grow heavier with each passing moment, as if laden with the burdens of her past and the shadows that lurked in the corners of her mind.

As she approached the familiar figure of Mr. Thompson, the custodian, Ava plastered on a warm smile that didn't quite reach her eyes. "Good morning, Mr. Thompson," she called out, her voice carrying a forced cheerfulness that belied the unease churning in her stomach.

Mr. Thompson turned, his weathered face creasing into a genial smile. "Mornin', Ms. Jennings. Another early start for the PTA, I see."

Ava nodded, her grip tightening on the box. "Always more to do," she replied, her tone light but her thoughts racing. How long could she keep up this facade of normalcy? How long before the cracks in her carefully constructed image began to show?

"Well, don't work too hard now," Mr. Thompson advised, his words echoing in the stillness of the hallway.

Ava forced a chuckle, the sound brittle and hollow. "I'll try not to," she promised, even as she knew it was a lie. The work was her sanctuary, her penance for sins she couldn't quite name but felt keenly in the depths of her soul.

As she continued down the corridor, the click of her heels against the linoleum floor seemed to mock her, a sinister metronome counting down to some inevitable doom. The PTA office loomed ahead, a beacon of normalcy in the gathering gloom of her thoughts.

Ava paused at the threshold, her hand hovering over the doorknob. For a moment, she allowed herself to imagine turning back, fleeing from the responsibilities and expectations that threatened to suffocate her. But the moment passed, as it always did, and she pushed open the door, stepping into the role she had crafted for herself with painstaking care.

The box of supplies landed on the desk with a dull thud, and Ava began to unpack, each item a piece in the elaborate puzzle of her life. As she worked, she couldn't shake the feeling that something was watching her, waiting for her to make a fatal misstep. But she pushed on, determined to maintain the illusion of the perfect PTA president, even as the shadows of her past threatened to engulf her.

The office door creaked open, revealing Principal Davis's imposing silhouette. Ava's breath caught in her throat, her fingers instinctively tightening around the stapler she held. The room seemed to shrink, the walls closing in as Principal Davis stepped inside, his stern gaze sweeping over her.

"Mrs. Jennings," he intoned, his voice a low rumble that sent shivers down Ava's spine. "I hope I'm not interrupting."

Ava forced a smile, the muscles in her face straining against the effort. "Not at all, Principal Davis. I was just..." she trailed off, gesturing vaguely at the scattered supplies.

Principal Davis nodded, his eyes flickering to the photos lining the walls. Frozen faces of past students stared back, their eyes seeming to follow Ava as she moved. Awards glinted dully in the harsh fluorescent light, each one a testament to the school's success – and to the weight of expectations that pressed down on Ava's shoulders.

"I wanted to express my gratitude," Principal Davis said, his words carefully measured. "Your dedication to this school, to the PTA – it's truly remarkable."

Ava's heart raced. Was this praise genuine, or merely a prelude to some darker revelation? She searched Principal Davis's face for any sign of deception, but found only the same inscrutable expression he always wore.

"Thank you," she managed, her voice barely above a whisper. "It's my pleasure to serve the community."

Principal Davis took a step closer, and Ava fought the urge to retreat. "You're a pillar of this community, Mrs. Jennings. We're fortunate to have you."

As he spoke, Ava couldn't shake the feeling that there was something lurking beneath his words, some hidden meaning she couldn't quite grasp. She nodded mechanically, her mind racing with possibilities, each more terrifying than the last.

"Is there anything else you need from me?" she asked, desperate to end this encounter before her mask of composure cracked completely.

Principal Davis paused, his gaze boring into her. For a moment, Ava was certain he could see right through her, could perceive the darkness that writhed just beneath her carefully constructed facade.

"No," he said at last. "That will be all. Carry on, Mrs. Jennings."

As he turned to leave, Ava released a breath she hadn't realized she'd been holding. The door closed behind him with a soft click, leaving her alone once more with her thoughts and the watchful eyes of the past that surrounded her.

Ava's trembling hands betrayed her as she arranged the chairs in neat rows, each scrape against the linoleum floor echoing like a scream in the empty room. The projector loomed before her, a cyclopean eye waiting to expose her secrets to the world. She fumbled with the cords, her fingers clumsy and cold.

"What if they see through me?" she thought, her heart racing. "What if they know what I've done?"

The door creaked open, startling Ava from her spiraling thoughts. A group of teachers entered, their laughter a jarring counterpoint to the dread that clung to her like a shroud.

"Ava! You're a godsend," chirped Ms. Reeves, her smile too bright, too trusting.

"Just doing my part," Ava replied, her voice hollow to her own ears.

The teachers gathered around her, their admiration palpable. It made her skin crawl.

"I don't know how you do it all," Mr. Hanson said, shaking his head in wonder.

Ava forced a smile, tasting ash. "It's nothing, really."

As they chattered, Ava's mind wandered to darker places. How long could she keep up this charade? How long before the mask slipped and they saw the monster beneath?

"Earth to Ava," Ms. Reeves laughed, waving a hand in front of her face. "Where'd you go?"

"Sorry," Ava murmured, "Just lost in thought about the meeting."

But her thoughts were elsewhere, in a place of shadows and regret, where the sins of her past waited patiently to devour her whole.

Mrs. Thompson's weathered hand brushed Ava's arm, jolting her from her reverie. The older woman's eyes, warm yet knowing, seemed to pierce through Ava's carefully constructed facade.

"You're doing marvelous work, dear," Mrs. Thompson murmured, her voice a soothing balm that only intensified Ava's guilt. "But remember, even the strongest pillars need support sometimes."

Ava swallowed hard, forcing a smile that felt like shattered glass. "Thank you, Mrs. Thompson. I... I appreciate that."

"We all have our burdens," the older teacher continued, her gaze unnervingly perceptive. "But sharing them can lighten the load."

A chill crept up Ava's spine. Did she know? Could she sense the darkness that lurked beneath Ava's polished exterior?

"I should greet the parents," Ava said abruptly, desperate to escape the suffocating kindness.

She hurried from the room, her heels echoing like accusatory whispers down the empty hallway. Outside, the crisp morning air did little to quell the panic rising in her chest.

Parents and children streamed towards the school entrance, their faces a blur of innocence and trust. Ava plastered on her warmest smile, a mask she'd perfected over years of deception.

"Good morning, Mrs. Jennings!" a cheerful voice called out.

Ava turned, her practiced grin hiding the torment within. "Welcome to another wonderful day at Pine View," she chirped, the lie tasting bitter on her tongue.

As she doled out high-fives and reassuring nods, Ava's mind raced. How long could she maintain this charade? How long before her past caught up with her, shattering the idyllic world she'd so carefully constructed?

The bell rang, its shrill cry like a harbinger of doom. Ava watched the last of the children disappear into the building, feeling the weight of her secrets pressing down upon her like a smothering shroud.

A woman with nervous eyes and fidgeting hands approached, breaking Ava's spiral of dread. "Mrs. Jennings? I'm Elena Rodriguez, Jamie's mom. I'm new here and—"

"Of course, Mrs. Rodriguez," Ava interrupted, her voice honey-sweet despite the acid churning in her stomach. "How can I help you?"

As Mrs. Rodriguez stumbled through a question about the upcoming fall festival, Ava's mind drifted to darker places. How easy it would be to manipulate this woman's trust, to exploit her vulnerability. The thought sent a perverse thrill through her, quickly followed by a wave of self-loathing.

"—so I was wondering if there's a way to volunteer?" Mrs. Rodriguez finished, hope etched across her face.

Ava's smile never faltered. "Absolutely. We always need helping hands." She outlined the various roles available, her words dripping with false enthusiasm. All the while, her inner voice hissed, Liar. Fraud. They'd despise you if they knew.

"Thank you so much," Mrs. Rodriguez gushed. "You've been so helpful."

If only you knew, Ava thought bitterly. Aloud, she said, "My pleasure. We're all family here at Pine View."

As Mrs. Rodriguez walked away, a group of children bounded past. Ava high-fived them mechanically, her practiced words of encouragement ringing hollow in her ears. "Great job on that science project, Tyler!" she called out, wondering if the boy could sense the hollowness behind her praise.

Each interaction was a fresh torment, a reminder of the chasm between her carefully crafted persona and the darkness that festered within. The children's laughter echoed like mocking jeers, their innocence a stark contrast to her own corrupted soul.

As the last stragglers hurried into the building, Ava stood alone on the steps, her smile fading like a dying star. The weight of her deceit pressed down upon her, a suffocating blanket of lies and half-truths. How long could she maintain this facade before it all came crashing down?

The staff lounge door creaked open, a gaping maw swallowing Ava whole. Inside, laughter mingled with the acrid scent of burnt coffee. Teachers huddled in conspiratorial clusters, their voices hushed yet piercing.

"Ava! Come, join us," Mrs. Thompson beckoned, her weathered face a map of false kindness. Ava's feet moved of their own accord, propelling her towards the group.

"How's the science fair shaping up?" Mr. Daniels inquired, his eyes gleaming with barely concealed schadenfreude.

Ava's lips curved upward, a practiced motion. "Brilliantly," she lied, her voice a sickly-sweet poison. "The children's enthusiasm is... infectious."

Laughter rippled through the group, a discordant melody that set Ava's teeth on edge. She listened as they shared classroom anecdotes, each story a dagger twisting in her gut. Their camaraderie was a cruel reminder of her own isolation.

"Speaking of infectious," Mrs. Thompson interjected, "that PTA meeting is starting soon, isn't it?"

Ava's smile tightened. "Indeed. Duty calls."

She excused herself, fleeing the suffocating camaraderie. The hallway stretched before her, a gauntlet of fluorescent lights and judgment. With each step towards the meeting room, dread coiled tighter in her chest.

Parents filled the chairs, their expectant gazes boring into her as she took her place at the podium. Ava's voice rang out, steady and assured, belying the tremor in her hands.

"Welcome, everyone. We have an exciting agenda tonight..."

Her words flowed effortlessly, a river of false promises and hollow enthusiasm. She outlined upcoming events, her passion a masterful performance that stirred the crowd. They hung on her every word, oblivious to the void that yawned behind her eyes.

As applause filled the room, Ava's inner voice whispered, They'll see through you eventually. It's only a matter of time.

As the last echoes of applause faded, Ava found herself alone in the emptied meeting room. Shadows crept along the walls, stretching like grasping fingers. She sank into a nearby chair, the weight of the day pressing down on her shoulders.

"Another successful performance," she murmured, her voice barely a whisper in the stillness.

Ava's gaze drifted to the window, where twilight painted the sky in bruised hues. A sense of accomplishment mingled with an undercurrent of unease, like oil and water refusing to mix.

"Why can't I shake this feeling?" she wondered, her fingers tracing abstract patterns on the tabletop.

Images from the day flashed through her mind: smiling faces, grateful parents, children's laughter. Each memory should have warmed her heart, yet a chill persisted.

As if summoned by her unease, a car pulled into the parking lot. The sleek black vehicle stood out starkly against the fading light. Ava's breath caught in her throat as a familiar figure emerged.

"Evelyn," she whispered, the name tasting of ash on her tongue.

Even from a distance, Evelyn Summers' polished appearance radiated an aura of menace. She strode towards the school entrance with purposeful steps, her designer heels clicking a rhythm of impending doom.

Ava's hand trembled as she reached for her phone. "I should warn the principal," she thought, but her fingers hovered motionless over the screen.

The satisfaction of the day's accomplishments crumbled like sand, leaving behind a desolate landscape of apprehension. In that moment, Ava knew with chilling certainty that her carefully constructed world was about to be tested.

"What fresh hell are you bringing this time, Evelyn?" Ava murmured, her words lost in the encroaching darkness.

Chapter 2

The crisp autumn air nipped at Ava's fingers as she arranged construction paper turkeys on the bulletin board outside Mrs. Hawkins' second-grade classroom. A chill crept up her spine, carrying whispers of dread she couldn't quite place. She shook it off, focusing on smoothing out a crooked feather.

"Almost time for the bell," Ava murmured, glancing at her watch. The hallways would soon flood with chattering children, their innocence a stark contrast to the shadows that seemed to lurk in every corner of Pine View Elementary.

As if summoned by her thoughts, a lone figure appeared at the end of the corridor. Oliver Summers, his backpack nearly as big as he was, shuffled towards her with downcast eyes.

"Good morning, Oliver," Ava called, her voice echoing off the empty walls. "You're cutting it a bit close today."

The boy's head snapped up, blue eyes wide with surprise. "Oh! Hi, Mrs. Jennings. I... I overslept."

Ava's heart clenched at the shame in his voice. Poor child, she thought. What burdens does he carry?

"Not to worry," she said, forcing cheer into her tone. "Let's get you to class before—"

The shrill ring of the bell cut her off, followed by the thunderous sound of doors slamming shut. Oliver's face crumpled as he realized he was locked out.

Ava's mind raced. She should open the door, let him in. But something held her back, a creeping unease that whispered of consequences. What if this simple act set something terrible in motion?

"Mrs. Jennings?" Oliver's voice quavered. "Can you... can you let me in?"

Ava's hand hovered over the doorknob, trembling. The metal felt ice-cold beneath her palm, as if warning her away. But she couldn't leave him out here, alone and afraid.

Could she?

Oliver's small fists began to pound against the door, the hollow thuds echoing through the empty hallway. "Help! Please, someone let me in!" His voice cracked, panic rising with each desperate plea.

Ava's heart raced, her chest tightening as she watched the boy's distress unfold. The sound of his frantic knocking seemed to reverberate in her very bones, each impact a reminder of her inaction.

"I shouldn't," she whispered to herself, even as her feet carried her towards the door. "What if this is a mistake?"

But Oliver's cries grew more frantic, his little body shaking with fear. "Mrs. Jennings! Are you there? Please help me!"

Ava's hand trembled as she reached for the lock. The metal felt unnaturally cold beneath her fingers, as if trying to warn her away. But she couldn't bear to see Oliver suffer any longer.

"It's alright, Oliver," she called out, her voice steadier than she felt. "I'm here. I'm opening the door now."

As the lock clicked open, a chill ran down Ava's spine. She couldn't shake the feeling that this simple act of kindness might lead to unforeseen consequences, dark tendrils of fate wrapping around them both.

The door swung open with an ominous creak, and Oliver stumbled in, his face tear-streaked and flushed. Ava's heart clenched at the sight of his trembling lip, her maternal instincts warring with the creeping dread that had taken root in her chest.

"There now, you're safe," she murmured, her voice barely above a whisper. But as she spoke, she became acutely aware of the sudden hush that had fallen over the schoolyard. Dozens of eyes bored into her back, a silent chorus of judgment.

Oliver sniffled, wiping his nose on his sleeve. "Thank you, Mrs. Jennings," he said, his voice small and quavering.

Before Ava could respond, a shrill voice cut through the air like a blade. "What in God's name do you think you're doing with my son?"

Evelyn Summers strode across the schoolyard, her heels clicking against the pavement with metronomic precision. Each step felt like a countdown to Ava's doom.

"Mrs. Summers, I—" Ava began, but Evelyn cut her off with a dismissive wave of her manicured hand.

"Save your excuses," Evelyn hissed, her eyes flashing with barely contained rage. "I saw everything. How dare you lock my boy out of the school? What kind of incompetent fool are you?"

Ava's mouth went dry, her thoughts scattered like leaves in a storm. She wanted to explain, to defend herself, but the words wouldn't come. Instead, she found herself transfixed by the malevolent gleam in Evelyn's eyes, a promise of retribution that chilled her to her very core.

Evelyn's voice dripped with venom as she leaned in close, her perfectly painted lips curling into a sneer. "I heard what you said about Oliver. Calling him 'slow.' Is that how you treat all the children under your care? Or just the ones you deem unworthy?"

The accusation hung in the air like a noxious cloud, suffocating Ava with its malice. Her heart pounded against her ribcage, a frantic drumbeat of confusion and dismay. She hadn't said anything of the sort. How could Evelyn twist a simple misunderstanding into such a vicious lie?

"Mrs. Summers, I assure you there's been a mistake," Ava managed, her voice trembling despite her efforts to remain calm. She could feel the weight of the onlookers' stares, their whispers a soft susurration of judgment. "I would never say such a thing about Oliver or any child."

But even as the words left her lips, Ava felt a creeping doubt. Had she said something that could have been misinterpreted? The memory of the past few minutes seemed to slip through her fingers like smoke, leaving only the acrid taste of uncertainty.

Evelyn's eyes narrowed, a predator sensing weakness. "Oh, I'm sure you wouldn't admit it now. But I know what I heard. And I promise you, Mrs. Jennings, this isn't over."

As Evelyn turned on her heel and stalked away, Ava was left with a gnawing sense of dread. The schoolyard suddenly felt vast and alien, a landscape of potential enemies. She wondered, with a shiver of foreboding, just how far Evelyn would go to see her fall.

Evelyn spun back around, her designer heels grinding against the concrete. Her eyes flashed with a fervor that bordered on madness. "You think you can just brush this off with your saccharine smile and empty platitudes?" she hissed, jabbing a manicured finger at Ava's chest.

Ava felt her breath catch, a cold tendril of fear wrapping around her heart. But she steeled herself, drawing on a well of inner strength she didn't know she possessed. "Mrs. Summers," she said, her voice low and steady, "I understand you're upset, but this isn't helping Oliver or anyone else."

"Don't you dare tell me what's best for my son!" Evelyn snarled, her face contorting with rage. "You're nothing but a glorified babysitter with delusions of grandeur. I'll see to it that you never work with children again."

The threat hung in the air, heavy and ominous. Ava could feel the eyes of the other parents and teachers boring into her, their silence a palpable weight. She wanted to shrink away, to disappear into the cracks of the schoolyard pavement. But she couldn't. She wouldn't.

"I've dedicated my life to these children," Ava said, her voice gaining strength. "I won't stand here and let you twist my words or my intentions. If you have concerns, we can discuss them civilly with the principal."

Evelyn's laugh was sharp and brittle. "Oh, we'll discuss it alright. With the school board, the superintendent, and every lawyer I can get my hands on."

As Evelyn's threats echoed in the schoolyard, Ava felt a strange calm settle over her. The world seemed to narrow, the cacophony of the morning fading to a distant hum. She knew, with a certainty that chilled her to her core, that this was only the beginning of a long and treacherous battle.

Ava's heart thundered in her chest, each beat a reminder of the precarious situation she now faced. The schoolyard had grown unnaturally still, as if the very air held its breath in anticipation of the next blow.

"You're making a terrible mistake, Mrs. Summers," Ava said, her voice barely above a whisper. The words tasted like ash in her mouth.

Evelyn's eyes glittered with malice. "Oh, I don't think so. The only mistake here is allowing someone like you near children."

A cold dread crept up Ava's spine. She could almost feel the tendrils of Evelyn's influence spreading, poisoning the community she'd worked so hard to nurture.

"This isn't over," Evelyn hissed, turning on her heel.

As Evelyn stalked away, Ava remained rooted to the spot, the weight of unspoken accusations pressing down on her. The curious, wary gazes of onlookers pierced her like daggers, and she wondered how many would stand with her when the storm truly hit.

The school bell rang, its cheerful tone a jarring contrast to the somber atmosphere. Ava watched as parents and children alike filed into the building, their whispers a soft, sinister undercurrent.

She took a deep, shuddering breath. The day stretched before her, long and foreboding, filled with the promise of more confrontations to come.

Chapter 3

The fluorescent lights flickered ominously as Ava approached Evelyn in the deserted school hallway. Shadows danced on the walls, mirroring the darkness that threatened to consume them both.

"Mrs. Summers," Ava said softly, her voice barely above a whisper. "I believe there's been a terrible misunderstanding."

Evelyn's eyes flashed with barely contained fury. The air grew thick with tension, suffocating in its intensity.

Ava swallowed hard, fighting the urge to flee. She had faced many challenges in her years at Pine View, but none quite like this. The weight of unspoken accusations pressed down upon her.

"I would never call Oliver slow," Ava continued, her words measured and careful. "It was an unintentional mistake, I assure you."

Evelyn's lips curled into a snarl. "Lies," she hissed, the single word dripping with venom. "All lies."

Ava's heart raced, pounding a frantic rhythm against her ribcage. She could feel the situation slipping away, like sand through an hourglass. Time was running out.

"Please, Mrs. Summers," Ava pleaded, reaching out a trembling hand. "I care deeply for all the children here. Oliver included."

But her words fell on deaf ears. Evelyn's face contorted, twisting into a mask of unbridled rage. The transformation was terrifying to behold.

"You neglectful, manipulative witch," Evelyn spat, each syllable a dagger aimed at Ava's heart. "I'll see you fired for this. Mark my words."

Ava recoiled, her back pressed against the cold lockers. The metal seeped through her clothing, chilling her to the bone. Or perhaps it was the ice in Evelyn's voice that froze her in place.

As Evelyn stormed away, her heels echoing like gunshots in the empty corridor, Ava was left alone with the ghosts of her past mistakes.

They whispered in her ear, taunting her with the promise of a future forever tainted by this moment.

The lights flickered once more, plunging the hallway into momentary darkness. When they sputtered back to life, Ava found herself wondering if the shadows had always been so long, so menacing. Or if, perhaps, they were simply a reflection of the darkness that now threatened to consume her very soul.

Ava's heart pounded against her ribcage as she scanned the bustling hallway. The cacophony of student chatter and slamming lockers seemed to fade into a dull roar, her focus narrowing on Evelyn's retreating form.

"Mrs. Summers," Ava called out, her voice barely above a whisper. She cleared her throat and tried again. "Mrs. Summers, please. We should discuss this privately."

Evelyn whirled around, her eyes flashing with barely contained fury. Ava gestured towards an empty classroom, her hand trembling slightly. "In here, perhaps?"

As they entered the room, the door clicked shut behind them with an ominous finality. Ava's skin prickled, a chill running down her spine despite the warmth of the afternoon sun streaming through the windows.

"Mrs. Summers," Ava began, her voice steady despite the turmoil within. "I understand your concerns, but I assure you—"

"Assure me?" Evelyn interrupted, her voice dripping with venom. "Your assurances mean nothing to me."

Ava took a deep breath, willing her racing thoughts to slow. How could she make Evelyn understand? The weight of her responsibility to the children, to the school, pressed down on her like a physical force.

"I've dedicated my life to this school," Ava said softly, her eyes meeting Evelyn's. "To these children. Every decision I make, every action I take, is with their best interests at heart."

But even as the words left her lips, Ava felt a creeping doubt. Had she truly done enough? Or were her efforts merely a façade, hiding a deeper, darker truth about her own inadequacies?

Evelyn's laugh was harsh, cutting through the air like shattered glass. "Manipulative to the end, aren't you?" she sneered, her perfectly manicured nails digging into her palms. "You weave pretty words, but I see through your deceit, Ava Jennings."

The accusation hung in the air, heavy and suffocating. Ava's heart raced, each beat a painful reminder of her vulnerability. She opened her mouth to protest, but Evelyn pressed on relentlessly.

"You're the root of all Oliver's troubles," Evelyn hissed, her eyes glittering with malice. "Your negligence, your incompetence - it's destroying my son's future."

Ava's mind reeled, memories of Oliver's struggles flashing before her eyes. Had she truly failed him so completely? The doubt gnawed at her, a festering wound in her psyche.

"Mrs. Summers, please," Ava whispered, her voice barely audible. "This isn't helping Oliver. We need to find a way to work together."

But Evelyn's face twisted into a mask of contempt. "Work together? With you? Never."

In that moment, Ava knew. The chasm between them was too vast, too deep to bridge with words alone. She swallowed hard, steeling herself for what must come next.

"Then perhaps," Ava said, her voice steadier than she felt, "we should involve Principal Davis. He can mediate, help us find a resolution that benefits everyone - especially Oliver."

As the words left her lips, Ava felt a chill of foreboding. What dark turns awaited them in the principal's office? What ghosts of past mistakes would rise to haunt them all?

The hollow echo of their footsteps reverberated through the empty hallway, a discordant rhythm that matched the frantic pounding of Ava's heart. Beside her, Evelyn's rage simmered, a palpable force that seemed to warp the very air around them. Ava's mind raced, memories of past confrontations flitting through her consciousness like restless specters.

"You won't get away with this," Evelyn hissed, her voice barely above a whisper. "I'll see you ruined, do you hear me?"

Ava's breath caught in her throat, but she forced herself to maintain her composure. "Mrs. Summers, please. Let's allow Principal Davis to help us resolve this."

As they approached the office, the door swung open, revealing Principal Davis's familiar silhouette. His warm smile did little to dispel the chill that had settled in Ava's bones.

"Ladies," he greeted, his tone gentle but firm. "Please, come in."

Ava hesitated at the threshold, a sudden wave of dread washing over her. What dark truths would be unveiled within these walls? What judgments would be passed?

Principal Davis gestured towards two chairs facing his desk. "Now, why don't you both tell me what's troubling you?"

As Ava sank into her seat, she couldn't shake the feeling that she was descending into the depths of her own personal hell, with Evelyn as her merciless tormentor and Principal Davis as the unwitting arbiter of her fate.

Evelyn's eyes flashed with a manic gleam as she leapt from her chair, her carefully manicured hands clutching the edge of Principal Davis's desk. "This woman," she spat, jabbing a finger towards Ava, "is a menace to our children!"

Ava's heart thundered in her chest, each beat a reminder of her vulnerability. She watched, paralyzed, as Evelyn's tirade unfolded like a nightmare given form.

"She's incompetent, negligent, and a danger to every student in this school," Evelyn continued, her voice rising to a fever pitch. "My Oliver—my precious boy—has suffered because of her carelessness!"

Principal Davis raised a hand, his brow furrowed. "Mrs. Summers, please—"

But Evelyn was relentless, her words a torrent of venom. "She should be fired immediately! Banned from ever working with children again!"

"That's quite enough," Principal Davis interjected, his tone sharper now. "Mrs. Summers, I must insist you maintain a respectful tone."

Ava's mind reeled, memories of past accusations swirling like leaves in a storm. She took a deep breath, steeling herself. This was her moment—perhaps her last chance.

"Principal Davis," she began, her voice steady despite the tremor in her hands, "I understand Mrs. Summers' concerns, but I assure you, they're unfounded."

Evelyn scoffed, but Ava pressed on, determination etched in every line of her face. "For years, I've dedicated myself to this school, to these children. Every decision I make is with their best interests at heart."

As she spoke, Ava could feel the weight of her words, each one a testament to her commitment. But would it be enough to dispel the shadows Evelyn had cast?

Principal Davis leaned back in his chair, the leather creaking ominously in the tense silence. His eyes, shadowed beneath furrowed brows, flicked between Ava and Evelyn. The ticking of the old clock on the wall seemed to grow louder, each second stretching into eternity.

"Ladies," he finally spoke, his voice low and measured, "I acknowledge the gravity of this situation." He turned to Evelyn, whose eyes glittered with barely contained fury. "Mrs. Summers, I assure you, we will investigate this matter thoroughly."

Ava's heart clenched, a cold dread seeping through her veins. Would her years of dedication crumble under the weight of Evelyn's accusations?

Principal Davis continued, his tone softening slightly, "However, Mrs. Summers, I urge you to consider the possibility of a misunderstanding."

Evelyn's lips curled into a sneer. "Misunderstanding? There's no misunderstanding when it comes to my son's well-being."

"Nevertheless," Principal Davis insisted, "we must approach this objectively."

As they rose to leave, Ava caught a glimpse of her reflection in the window – a pale ghost, haunted by unspoken fears. She forced a smile, clinging to a fragile hope that Principal Davis's intervention might quell the storm.

But one look at Evelyn's face, contorted with unyielding determination, shattered that illusion. This was far from over, and Ava knew the true nightmare was only beginning.

Ava's footsteps echoed hollowly through the empty hallways of Pine View Elementary, each step a painful reminder of her precarious position. The once-welcoming corridors now felt like a gauntlet, lined with unseen eyes judging her every move.

She paused before the door to the volunteer room, her hand trembling as it hovered over the handle. Taking a deep breath, she steeled herself and entered.

"Good morning, everyone," Ava said, forcing cheer into her voice. The other volunteers turned, their smiles not quite reaching their eyes. Had word already spread?

As she sorted through a stack of papers, her mind raced. I can't let this break me. The children need me.

"Ava?" Mrs. Chen, another long-time volunteer, approached cautiously. "Are you... alright?"

Ava's smile faltered. "Of course, why wouldn't I be?"

Mrs. Chen hesitated. "It's just... there are these flyers..."

A chill ran down Ava's spine. "What flyers?"

Before Mrs. Chen could answer, a commotion erupted in the hallway. Ava rushed out to find walls plastered with garish pink papers, Evelyn's perfectly manicured hand tacking up more.

"What are you doing?" Ava's voice cracked.

Evelyn turned, her eyes gleaming with malicious triumph. "Protecting our children from monsters like you."

Ava's gaze fell on the flyers, each a dagger to her heart:

"DANGER: AVA JENNINGS – CHILD ABUSER!"

"UNFIT TO BE NEAR CHILDREN!"

"LIAR AND MANIPULATOR!"

The world spun, darkness creeping at the edges of Ava's vision. How had it come to this?

Ava stumbled away from the cacophony of whispers and accusatory glances, her legs carrying her through the school's winding corridors like a wraith. The once-welcoming halls now seemed to close in, suffocating her with each step.

She found herself at Mrs. Thompson's classroom door, her trembling hand rapping softly against the worn wood.

"Come in," came the familiar, warm voice.

Ava slipped inside, her composure crumbling as she met Mrs. Thompson's concerned gaze. "Oh, Ava," the older woman breathed, quickly crossing the room to embrace her.

"I don't know how much more I can take," Ava whispered, her voice raw with unshed tears. "Evelyn's lies... they're everywhere."

Mrs. Thompson guided her to a chair, her touch gentle but firm. "Remember, dear, this too shall pass. The truth has a way of coming to light."

Ava's laugh was bitter, hollow. "But at what cost? My reputation? My passion for helping these children?"

"Your strength," Mrs. Thompson countered, her blue eyes piercing. "is not measured by the absence of struggle, but by how you face it."

As Ava absorbed these words, a flicker of determination kindled within her. Perhaps, she thought, the darkness hasn't won yet.

Chapter 4

The classroom door creaked open, a sound like bones snapping. Ava slipped inside, her chest tight with dread. The fluorescent lights cast sickly shadows across Mrs. Thompson's desk, where papers lay strewn like entrails.

"Ava, dear?" Mrs. Thompson's voice drifted through the gloom. "Is everything alright?"

Ava's lips twitched, struggling to form a smile. "Oh, just peachy," she lied, her words dripping with false cheer.

Mrs. Thompson's blue eyes narrowed, seeing through the facade. "You look as though you've seen a ghost."

If only it were just a ghost, Ava thought bitterly. Evelyn's accusations echoed in her mind, a cacophony of cruel whispers. She was everywhere and nowhere, haunting Ava's every step.

"I'm fine, really," Ava insisted, her voice hollow. "Just a bit tired."

But exhaustion couldn't explain away the pallor of her skin or the tremor in her hands. Mrs. Thompson rose from her chair, concern etched into the lines of her face.

"My dear, you're shaking like a leaf," she murmured. "What's troubling you?"

Ava's carefully constructed mask began to crack. How could she explain the campaign of terror waged against her? The whispered rumors, the pointed fingers, the cold stares that followed her through the school halls?

"It's nothing," Ava whispered, but the words tasted like ash on her tongue. "Nothing at all."

Ava sank into the chair across from Mrs. Thompson, her fingers interlacing and twisting like pale, restless serpents. The room seemed to shrink, shadows creeping in from the corners, as if eager to witness her unraveling.

"It's Evelyn," she began, her voice a brittle whisper. "She's... she's become a nightmare made flesh."

Mrs. Thompson leaned forward, her gentle blue eyes now pools of concern in the dim light. "Tell me everything, dear," she urged softly.

Ava's words spilled out like a dark tide, each revelation more chilling than the last. "She's turned the entire PTA against me. Whispers in hallways, accusations of favoritism, hints of impropriety. It's as if she's poisoned the very air we breathe."

As she spoke, Ava's mind drifted to the confrontation in the parking lot, Evelyn's face contorted with a hatred so pure it seemed otherworldly. "She cornered me yesterday, her words like daggers. 'I'll see you ruined,' she hissed. 'Your precious reputation in tatters.'"

Mrs. Thompson listened, her face a mask of empathy tinged with growing horror. "Oh, Ava," she breathed, "I had no idea it had gone this far."

But Ava wasn't finished. The floodgates had opened, and the torrent of her anguish would not be stemmed. "And now the complaints are rolling in. Fabricated grievances, each more absurd than the last. But in their sheer volume, they take on a life of their own."

She paused, a humorless laugh escaping her lips. "It's almost admirable, really. The artistry of her malice."

Mrs. Thompson reached out, her weathered hand gently enveloping Ava's trembling fingers. The touch, warm and reassuring, sent a shiver through Ava's spine - a stark contrast to the icy dread that had taken root in her chest.

"My dear," Mrs. Thompson murmured, her voice a soothing balm in the suffocating silence of the classroom, "you are not alone in this darkness."

Ava's eyes, brimming with unshed tears, met Mrs. Thompson's gaze. She saw reflected there a strength she desperately needed, a lifeline in the tempest of her fears.

"I-I'm terrified," Ava confessed, her voice quavering like a leaf in an autumn gale. "If I lose this position... it's not just a title. It's everything I've worked for, everything I believe in."

The words tumbled out, each one carrying the weight of her despair. "The children, Mrs. Thompson. The community. They need someone who cares, who fights for them. If Evelyn wins... if she takes this from me..."

Ava's voice trailed off, lost in the yawning chasm of potential loss. In her mind's eye, she saw the school playground empty, devoid of the laughter and joy she had worked so hard to cultivate. The image was a dagger to her heart.

"What if," she whispered, the words barely audible, "what if she's already won?"

Mrs. Thompson leaned forward, her weathered hands still clasping Ava's. The ancient wooden chair creaked beneath her, a mournful sound that echoed through the dim classroom. Shadows danced across her face, casting her gentle features in an eerie light.

"My child," she began, her voice a hushed whisper that seemed to caress the very air, "integrity is a beacon in the darkest of nights. It guides us when all other lights have gone out."

Ava felt a chill run down her spine, Mrs. Thompson's words weaving a spell around her. She leaned in, drawn by an inexplicable force.

"Years ago," Mrs. Thompson continued, her eyes taking on a faraway look, "I faced a parent who sought to destroy everything I had built. She was a vengeful spirit, much like your Evelyn."

Ava's eyes widened, her breath catching in her throat. She had never imagined Mrs. Thompson, always so composed, facing such torment.

"What... what did you do?" Ava asked, her voice barely above a whisper.

A ghost of a smile flickered across Mrs. Thompson's face. "I stood firm, my dear. I refused to let her hatred poison my soul. And in the end, her own darkness consumed her."

Ava felt a shiver of realization course through her. The room seemed to darken further, the shadows growing longer, more menacing. Yet within her, a small flame of hope began to flicker.

"Remember," Mrs. Thompson intoned, her voice taking on an almost otherworldly quality, "in the face of malevolence, your true self is your strongest armor."

Mrs. Thompson's blue eyes, once gentle, now bore into Ava with an intensity that made her skin prickle. "Document everything, Ava," she whispered, her voice low and urgent. "Every whispered accusation, every poisonous rumor. Let the truth be your shield against Evelyn's venom."

Ava's heart quickened, the weight of Mrs. Thompson's words settling like lead in her stomach. She imagined Evelyn's polished nails, sharp as talons, tearing at her reputation. "But how..." she began, her voice trembling.

"A journal," Mrs. Thompson interjected, sliding a leather-bound book across the desk. Its cover was worn, the pages yellowed with age. "Record it all. Let no detail, however small, escape your notice."

Ava's fingers brushed the journal, a spark of electricity seeming to pass between her and the object. She could almost feel the whispers of past secrets trapped within its pages.

"And remember," Mrs. Thompson added, her voice barely audible, "in this battle, you are not alone."

A newfound determination blazed in Ava's eyes, chasing away the shadows that had threatened to engulf her. She nodded, clutching the journal to her chest like a talisman against the darkness that Evelyn represented.

"I understand," Ava breathed, feeling as though she had just been initiated into some ancient, secret society of survivors. The room seemed to pulse around her, alive with unspoken histories of triumph over malevolence.

Mrs. Thompson's blue eyes flickered with an otherworldly light as she leaned forward, her voice a haunting whisper. "Ava, my dear, you've touched so many lives here. The children... they bloom under your care like flowers in a forgotten garden."

Ava's breath caught, memories of smiling faces and tiny hands reaching for hers flashing through her mind like specters. "But Evelyn..." she murmured, her voice quavering.

"Evelyn is but a passing storm," Mrs. Thompson intoned, her words carrying the weight of ancient wisdom. "You are the bedrock of this community, Ava. The very foundation upon which our hopes are built."

A chill ran down Ava's spine, both terrifying and exhilarating. She rose from her chair, her legs trembling beneath her. "I... I won't let them down," she vowed, her voice growing stronger with each word.

Mrs. Thompson's smile was enigmatic, almost knowing. "Of course you won't, my dear. The spirits of those who came before us watch over you."

Ava clutched the journal tighter, feeling as if she'd been granted some arcane power. "Thank you," she breathed, turning to leave. "I'll face her. I'll face them all."

As she reached the door, Mrs. Thompson's voice drifted to her once more, soft as a death rattle. "Remember, Ava. In the darkest night, we find our truest selves."

Ava stepped into the shadowy hallway, her heart pounding with renewed purpose and an inexplicable sense of dread.

Chapter 5

The shrill ring of the phone pierced the gloomy silence of the precinct. Officer Maria Ramirez's hand hovered over the receiver, a chill creeping up her spine. Something wicked this way comes, she thought, her intuition rarely led her astray.

"Officer Ramirez speaking," she answered, her voice steady despite the foreboding in her gut.

"Maria, we've got a live one for you," came the gravelly voice of Sergeant Thompson. "Evelyn Summers just filed a complaint against an Ava Jennings. Accusations of stalking and attempted harm."

Maria's brow furrowed, her mind racing. Evelyn Summers - that name carried weight, dripping with influence and barely concealed malice. And Ava Jennings? The kind-hearted teacher whose reputation preceded her? An unlikely pairing, to be sure.

"Give me the details, Sarge," Maria commanded, her pen poised over her notepad. As Thompson rattled off dates and times, Maria's hand moved mechanically, jotting down the information. But her thoughts wandered to darker places. What secrets lay buried beneath this pristine suburban veneer?

"Summers claims Jennings has been following her son to and from school, leaving threatening notes in his backpack," Thompson continued, his voice tinged with skepticism. "Says she fears for both their lives."

Maria's lips tightened. Fear, or fabrication? The line between the two often blurred in cases like these, where emotions ran high and reason took a backseat to primal instincts.

"Anything else?" Maria probed, sensing there was more lurking beneath the surface.

"Yeah," Thompson sighed, "Summers wants Jennings arrested immediately. Says she has evidence, but won't disclose what it is until you're face to face."

Of course she wouldn't, Maria mused. The puppetmaster always holds the strings close to her chest. "I'll head over to the school now," she said, already rising from her desk.

As she hung up the phone, a heaviness settled over Maria. This case reeked of hidden agendas and long-buried grudges. But whose sins would be unearthed in the process? And at what cost?

The answers, she knew, lay in the shadows cast by Pine View Elementary's cheerful facade. It was time to step into the darkness and see what monsters lurked within.

The autumn sun cast long, skeletal shadows across the parking lot as Officer Maria Ramirez pulled up to Pine View Elementary. The cheerful mural adorning the school's facade seemed to mock the grim purpose of her visit, its vibrant colors a stark contrast to the murky waters she was about to wade into.

As she strode through the double doors, the sterile scent of disinfectant assaulted her nostrils, mingling with the underlying musk of fear that seemed to permeate the air. The hallways echoed with the distant laughter of children, a haunting melody that sent a chill down Maria's spine.

"Can I help you?" The receptionist's voice, saccharine sweet, cut through Maria's thoughts like a knife.

"Officer Ramirez," she replied, flashing her badge. "I need to speak with Ava Jennings."

The receptionist's smile faltered for a moment, a flicker of something - concern? complicity? - passing behind her eyes. "Of course," she chirped, her cheerfulness now strained. "Ms. Jennings' office is down the hall, third door on the left."

As Maria made her way down the corridor, her mind raced. What secrets lay hidden behind these brightly decorated walls? What darkness lurked beneath the veneer of suburban bliss?

She paused outside Ava's office, her hand hovering over the doorknob. The weight of unseen eyes pressed upon her, as if the very building itself was holding its breath, waiting to see what truths would be unveiled.

With a steadying breath, Maria steeled herself for what lay ahead. The monsters of the past were stirring, and it was her duty to drag them into the light - no matter how ugly the revelation might be.

Maria rapped her knuckles against the door, the sound echoing like a death knell in the quiet hallway. She pushed it open, revealing Ava Jennings hunched over her desk, a sea of papers spread before her like the remnants of a shipwreck.

"Ms. Jennings?" Maria's voice cut through the stillness. "I'm Officer Ramirez."

Ava looked up, her kind eyes clouded with an unspoken weariness. "Officer? What can I do for you?"

Maria's fingers twitched, itching to reach for her notepad. Instead, she clasped her hands behind her back. "I'm here about a complaint filed by Evelyn Summers. She's accused you of stalking and attempting to harm her."

The color drained from Ava's face, leaving her as pale as the papers before her. "What? That's... that's absurd!" Her voice trembled, a leaf caught in an autumn gale.

Maria watched Ava closely, searching for any tell-tale signs of guilt. But all she saw was genuine shock, mixed with a hint of... was that fear?

Ava's hands fluttered like trapped birds as she spoke. "I've never... I would never harm anyone, especially not Evelyn or her son. This must be some kind of misunderstanding."

As Ava stumbled through her denial, Maria couldn't shake the feeling that something darker lurked beneath the surface of this quaint elementary school. The walls seemed to press in around them, whispering secrets that begged to be uncovered.

"Tell me your side of the story, Ms. Jennings," Maria urged, her voice low and steady. "What exactly is your relationship with Evelyn Summers?"

Ava's eyes darted to the window, where shadows of bare branches clawed at the glass. She drew a shaky breath, her words emerging like wisps of fog. "Evelyn and I... we were once friends. Or so I thought."

Officer Ramirez's pen scratched across her notepad, the sound eerily reminiscent of rats scurrying in the walls. "What changed?"

"It was gradual," Ava murmured, her gaze unfocused as if peering into a distant past. "Little things at first. Misunderstandings. Then accusations. She began to see threats where there were none."

Maria leaned forward, her chair creaking ominously. "Can you be more specific?"

Ava's fingers twisted in her lap, a silent dance of anxiety. "She claimed I was favoring other children over Oliver in school activities. That I was... poisoning the other parents against her."

The officer's eyes narrowed, probing for cracks in Ava's facade. "And were you?"

A bitter laugh escaped Ava's lips, startling in its harshness. "No. Never. But Evelyn... she sees the world through a warped lens. Everything is a conspiracy against her and Oliver."

Maria's pen paused, hovering over the paper like a guillotine blade. "I see. Ms. Jennings, I'll need to speak with Evelyn to hear her side of this... unfortunate situation."

Ava's face paled further, if that were possible. "Of course," she whispered, her voice barely audible over the mournful wind outside. "But please, you must understand. I'm not the monster she's painted me to be."

As Maria stood to leave, the shadows in the room seemed to lengthen, reaching out with grasping fingers. She couldn't shake the feeling that in this battle between Ava and Evelyn, there were no true innocents – only shades of guilt, as murky as the gathering storm clouds outside.

Officer Ramirez's gaze bore into Ava, her eyes dark pools of unreadable intent. "Ms. Jennings," she said, her voice low and measured,

"I need your full cooperation. Any evidence, any witnesses that could shed light on this... situation."

Ava felt a chill creep up her spine, despite the stuffy warmth of her small office. The walls seemed to press in, whispering accusations. She swallowed hard, her throat dry as parchment.

"Of course, Officer," Ava replied, her words barely above a whisper. "I want nothing more than to clear my name of these... these ghastly allegations."

With trembling hands, Ava reached for a notepad, her pen scratching against the paper like rats in the walls. Names flowed from her pen, a litany of potential saviors or inadvertent betrayers.

"Here," she said, tearing the page free and extending it towards Officer Ramirez. "Fellow teachers, parents... They were present during the times Evelyn claims I... I..."

Ava's voice trailed off, unable to voice the horrors Evelyn had accused her of. The silence hung heavy, pregnant with unspoken fears.

Officer Ramirez took the list, her eyes scanning the names. "And these individuals, they can corroborate your version of events?"

"I believe so," Ava replied, a flicker of hope kindling in her chest. But doubt, that insidious serpent, coiled around her heart. What if they had seen something she hadn't? What if her own memories were unreliable, tainted by the fog of stress and sleepless nights?

As Officer Ramirez folded the paper and tucked it away, Ava couldn't shake the feeling that she had just sealed her own fate, one way or another. The truth would out, but would it be enough to banish the shadows that now clung to her like a second skin?

Officer Ramirez's eyes softened, a momentary crack in her professional facade. "Thank you, Ms. Jennings. Your cooperation is... appreciated." The words hung in the air, hollow as a tomb. "We'll conduct a thorough investigation to uncover the truth."

Ava nodded, her throat constricting. The truth. What a fickle, elusive thing it had become.

As Officer Ramirez turned to leave, Ava's voice escaped her, unbidden. "And if the truth isn't enough?"

The officer paused, her hand on the doorknob. She didn't turn back. "Then we'll cross that bridge when we come to it."

The door clicked shut, leaving Ava alone with the echoes of her fears. Outside, footsteps receded down the hallway, each one a drumbeat of impending doom.

Ava's gaze drifted to the window, where gray clouds gathered like spectral onlookers. In the distance, a solitary figure stood motionless in the parking lot. Evelyn. Waiting. Watching.

A chill slithered down Ava's spine as Officer Ramirez's silhouette merged with Evelyn's. Two faces of justice, she thought. But whose truth would prevail?

Officer Ramirez approached the main office, her footsteps echoing in the empty corridor like a funeral march. Through the glass, she caught sight of Evelyn Summers, a statue of barely contained fury. Ramirez steeled herself, knowing the storm that awaited.

"Mrs. Summers?" Ramirez's voice cut through the oppressive silence. "I'm Officer Maria Ramirez. I'm here to discuss your complaint against Ms. Jennings."

Evelyn's eyes, cold as winter frost, locked onto Ramirez. "Finally," she hissed, her manicured nails digging into her designer handbag. "Someone willing to listen to reason."

Ramirez gestured towards an empty conference room. "Shall we?"

As they settled into the sterile space, Ramirez couldn't shake the feeling of entering a lion's den. "Mrs. Summers, I need to hear your side of the story. Any evidence you have would be helpful."

Evelyn's composure cracked, a dam bursting. "Evidence? How about the terror in my son's eyes every time that woman comes near? The 'chance' encounters at the grocery store, the park?" Her voice dripped venom. "She's everywhere, Officer. Watching. Waiting."

Ramirez jotted notes, her pen scratching a rhythm against the silence. "Can you provide specific instances, dates?"

"October 15th," Evelyn spat. "She cornered Oliver after school, whispering God knows what poison into his ears. When I confronted her, she smiled. Smiled! Like a cat that got the canary."

As Evelyn's tale unfolded, each word laced with vitriol, Ramirez found herself adrift in a sea of accusations. The truth, she realized, was as murky as the shadows that seemed to gather in the corners of the room.

"And the threats?" Ramirez probed, her voice steady despite the unease coiling in her gut.

Evelyn leaned forward, her eyes burning with a fervor that sent a chill down Ramirez's spine. "She said, and I quote, 'Your son is special, Mrs. Summers. It would be a shame if anything were to happen to him.'"

The words hung in the air, a noose tightening around an unseen neck. Ramirez fought to maintain her professional mask, even as doubt gnawed at her certainty.

"Thank you, Mrs. Summers," she managed, her mouth dry. "We'll investigate thoroughly."

As Ramirez stood to leave, Evelyn's hand shot out, gripping her wrist with surprising strength. "Don't let her fool you, Officer," she whispered, her voice thick with desperation. "Behind that mask of kindness lies a monster."

Ramirez nodded, extricating herself from Evelyn's grasp. As she stepped into the hallway, the weight of conflicting narratives pressed down upon her. In the distance, a child's laughter echoed, carefree and innocent. Ramirez couldn't help but wonder how long that innocence would last in a world where truth and lies danced so intimately.

Officer Ramirez's pen scratched across her notepad, the sound grating in the oppressive silence of the room. Evelyn's words hung heavy in the air, each accusation another layer of darkness settling over them.

"Mrs. Summers," Ramirez began, her voice low and measured, "can you provide any concrete evidence of these threats?"

Evelyn's eyes flashed, a tempest brewing behind her carefully composed facade. "Evidence? That woman is cunning, Officer. She leaves no trace."

Ramirez felt a flicker of doubt, a shadow passing over her certainty. She pressed on, "Any witnesses to these encounters?"

"My son," Evelyn hissed, leaning forward. "Oliver has seen her lurking, watching us. He's terrified."

The officer's mind raced, piecing together the fragments of truth and paranoia. Was this the raving of a delusional mother, or a genuine cry for help?

"And what about security footage?" Ramirez probed, her instincts prickling.

Evelyn's laugh was bitter, echoing in the small space. "Oh, she's too clever for that. Always just out of frame, always with an alibi."

As Ramirez jotted down notes, she couldn't shake the feeling that she was descending into a labyrinth of half-truths and unspoken fears. The case, like the room around them, seemed to grow darker with each passing moment.

Chapter 6

The shadows lengthened in Ava's cozy living room, stretching like grasping fingers across the floor. She paced, her steps echoing in the emptiness. Evelyn's latest threat reverberated in her mind, a cruel taunt that wouldn't fade.

"I'll destroy everything you hold dear, Ava. Everything."

Ava's hands trembled as she reached for her phone. How had it come to this? She'd only ever wanted to help, to make the school a better place. Now her world was crumbling, all because of one woman's twisted vendetta.

A name surfaced in her thoughts: Detective Marcus Johnson. She'd heard whispers of his reputation, a man who could unravel the most tangled webs of deceit. But would he believe her? Would anyone?

As if summoned by her desperate thoughts, a news segment flickered to life on her muted TV. There he was - Detective Johnson, his weathered face etched with determination as he addressed a crowd of reporters.

"Another case closed," the caption read. "Detective Johnson brings down notorious blackmail ring."

Ava's breath caught. She studied his stern features, the glint of steely resolve in his eyes. This man had faced down monsters before. Perhaps he could face down Evelyn.

But a chill crept up her spine. What if he saw through her? What if he uncovered the secrets she'd buried so deep, the ones that gnawed at her in the dark hours of the night?

No. She couldn't think like that. This was her last hope.

With trembling fingers, she dialed the police station's number. Each ring felt like an eternity, each moment of silence a judgment on her soul.

"Detective Johnson's office," a gruff voice answered.

Ava swallowed hard, her voice barely above a whisper. "Please... I need his help. It's a matter of life and death."

The truth of those words settled over her like a shroud. How long before Evelyn's threats became actions? How long before the darkness consuming her life spread to those she loved?

As she waited for a response, Ava's gaze drifted to the framed photo on her mantle - smiling faces, a happier time. She wondered, with a pang of dread, if she'd ever know such peace again.

The line crackled with a heavy sigh. "Detective Johnson speaking. What's this about life and death?"

Ava's words tumbled out, a torrent of fear and desperation. "I'm being threatened, stalked. She's everywhere, watching, waiting. I can't—"

"Slow down, ma'am," Johnson cut in, his tone laced with weary skepticism. "Who's threatening you?"

"Evelyn Summers," Ava whispered, the name tasting like poison on her tongue. "She's... she's relentless. Notes, calls, 'accidents' that aren't accidents. Please, I need—"

"Summers?" Johnson's voice sharpened. "The attorney's wife? Listen, Mrs...?"

"Jennings. Ava Jennings."

"Mrs. Jennings, these are serious allegations. Do you have concrete evidence?"

Ava's heart sank. She could hear the reluctance, the unspoken dismissal in his voice. "I... not exactly, but—"

"Then I'm afraid there's little I can do," Johnson said, his words clipped. "We deal in facts, not hunches or paranoia."

Paranoia. The word echoed in Ava's mind, mocking her. Was that all this was? Had Evelyn's torment driven her to madness?

No. She knew the truth, felt it in her bones. "Detective, please," she pleaded, hating the quaver in her voice. "Just... just meet with me. Let me explain. I swear, this is real."

Silence stretched between them, heavy with unspoken judgments. Ava held her breath, wondering if she'd already lost her last chance at salvation.

Ava's fingers tightened around the phone, her knuckles whitening. She couldn't let this opportunity slip away. "Detective Johnson," she began, her voice steadier now, "I understand your skepticism. But I'm not some hysterical woman crying wolf. I'm the PTA president at Pine View Elementary. I've dedicated my life to this community, to protecting our children. Now I need protection."

A low hum came from Johnson's end of the line. "Go on," he said, his tone guarded but attentive.

Ava seized the opening. "Evelyn's campaign against me is calculated, methodical. She's dismantling my life piece by piece. Yesterday, I found a dead bird on my doorstep, its wings arranged in the shape of a heart. The day before, all the tires on my car were slashed. This isn't paranoia, Detective. It's terror."

Johnson's breath hitched almost imperceptibly. "That's... disturbing," he admitted. "But why you? What's her motive?"

"I wish I knew," Ava replied, a chill creeping up her spine. "But I fear I'm not her first victim. There's a pattern here, a darkness that needs to be brought to light. And you, Detective, have a reputation for solving the unsolvable."

A long pause followed. Ava could almost hear the gears turning in Johnson's mind, weighing the risks against his innate curiosity.

Finally, he spoke. "Mrs. Jennings, I can't promise anything. But... I'm intrigued. Let's meet tomorrow, 9 AM, at Rosemary's Diner. We'll discuss this further."

Relief flooded through Ava, tinged with a flicker of hope. "Thank you, Detective. You won't regret this."

As she hung up, Ava gazed out her window at the gathering dusk. Shadows lengthened across her lawn, and for a moment, she thought she saw a figure standing beneath the old oak tree. But when she blinked, it was gone.

Tomorrow, she thought. Tomorrow, the hunt begins.

Detective Johnson hunched over his desk, the harsh fluorescent light casting deep shadows across his weathered face. A sea of documents lay before him, each a fragment of Evelyn Summers' past. His blue eyes darted from paper to paper, piecing together a mosaic of malevolence.

"Charitable donations, impeccable credit score, not so much as a parking ticket," he muttered, his voice a low growl. "Too clean. Nobody's this perfect."

Ava leaned forward, her fingers tracing the edge of a glossy photograph. "What about her social circles? Surely someone must have noticed something... off."

Johnson's gaze met hers, a flicker of admiration crossing his face. "Astute observation, Mrs. Jennings. I've compiled a list of Evelyn's associates over the past decade. Notice any familiar names?"

Ava's eyes widened as she scanned the document. "Rebecca Thornton... Sarah Palmer... They were both PTA presidents at different schools in the district. And they both resigned abruptly, citing 'personal reasons.'"

"Precisely," Johnson nodded, his voice taking on a grim tone. "And both moved out of state shortly after. Coincidence?"

Ava felt a chill creep up her spine. "You don't believe in coincidences, do you, Detective?"

"In my line of work, Mrs. Jennings, coincidences are often just patterns we haven't deciphered yet." He paused, his piercing gaze fixed on a point in the distance. "We need to contact these women. Discreetly."

As they worked, Ava couldn't shake the feeling of being watched. She glanced over her shoulder, half-expecting to see Evelyn's polished silhouette lurking in the shadows. The room suddenly felt smaller, the air thick with unspoken dread.

"Detective," Ava whispered, her voice barely audible, "what if we're already too late? What if Evelyn knows we're onto her?"

Johnson's face remained impassive, but Ava noticed his hand tighten ever so slightly on his pen. "Then we'd better work faster, Mrs. Jennings. The clock is ticking, and I fear the next move in this macabre game may already be in motion."

The air in Detective Johnson's dimly lit office grew heavy with foreboding as he slid a thick manila folder across the desk. Ava's trembling fingers traced the edge, hesitant to open it.

"Mrs. Jennings," Johnson's gravelly voice cut through the silence, "what you're about to see... it ain't pretty."

Ava swallowed hard, steeling herself as she flipped open the folder. Her eyes widened, horror etching itself across her features.

"Oh God," she whispered, her voice quavering.

Inside were photos - dozens of them. Shattered windshields, slashed tires, graffitied homes. But it was the faces that chilled Ava to her core. Men and women, their eyes haunted, their expressions a mixture of fear and defeat.

"Evelyn's handiwork," Johnson said, his tone flat. "Spanning back fifteen years. She's meticulous, patient. A predator playing the long game."

Ava's hands shook as she leafed through the documents. "How... how has she gotten away with this?"

Johnson leaned back, shadows dancing across his weathered face. "Money. Connections. And a knack for staying just this side of legal. But mainly? Fear. Her victims are too terrified to come forward."

A cold dread settled in Ava's stomach. "And now I'm on her list."

"We can't let that happen," Johnson said, leaning forward. "We need to outmaneuver her, Mrs. Jennings. Turn the tables."

Ava nodded, a spark of determination igniting in her eyes. "What's our next move?"

Johnson's lips curved into a grim smile. "We set a trap. But it's risky. You'll be the bait."

As they began to outline their plan, Ava couldn't shake the feeling that they were stepping into the lion's den. But what choice did she have? The alternative was unthinkable.

In the shadows of the office, the ghosts of Evelyn's past victims seemed to whisper a warning: "Be careful. She always wins in the end."

The early morning fog clung to Oakwood like a shroud, muffling footsteps and hushed voices. Ava stood before the wrought-iron gates of Evelyn's sprawling estate, her heart a frenetic drum in her chest. Detective Johnson's presence beside her was a cold comfort.

"Remember," he murmured, his eyes scanning the property, "we're here to gather information, not confront."

Ava nodded, swallowing hard. "What if she sees through our ruse?"

Johnson's lips tightened. "Then we improvise."

They approached the front door, its ornate knocker a snarling lion's head. Ava's knuckles whitened as she grasped it, the metal icy against her skin. Three sharp raps echoed through the house.

Footsteps approached, each one amplifying Ava's dread. The door creaked open, revealing Evelyn's polished facade.

"Mrs. Jennings," Evelyn purred, her smile a razor's edge. "To what do I owe this... pleasure?"

Ava forced a brittle smile. "We're conducting a neighborhood survey about school safety. May we come in?"

Evelyn's eyes narrowed, flickering between Ava and Johnson. For a heart-stopping moment, Ava feared their cover was blown. But then Evelyn's mask slipped back into place.

"Of course," she said, stepping aside. "How thoughtful of you to include me."

As they followed Evelyn into the lion's den, Ava caught Johnson's subtle nod. The trap was set. Now, they just had to survive long enough to spring it.

The air in Evelyn's study hung thick with the scent of old leather and hidden secrets. Ava's eyes darted across the room, searching for anything out of place, while Detective Johnson engaged their hostess in seemingly innocuous conversation.

"Quite the collection you have here," Johnson remarked, gesturing to a wall of framed photographs.

Evelyn's lips curled into a smug smile. "Yes, I do enjoy... preserving memories."

As Evelyn launched into a monologue about her charitable endeavors, Ava's gaze settled on a peculiar frame. Unlike the others, it was turned face-down on a side table. Her heart raced as she inched closer, fingers itching to reveal its contents.

"Mrs. Jennings?" Evelyn's sharp voice cut through the air. "Is everything alright?"

Ava's hand froze mid-reach. "Oh, I was just admiring your... lovely decor," she stammered, forcing a smile.

Johnson cleared his throat, drawing Evelyn's attention back to him. "You mentioned your involvement with the school board. How long have you held that position?"

As Evelyn preened under Johnson's feigned interest, Ava seized her chance. In one fluid motion, she flipped the frame over, barely stifling a gasp at what she saw.

It was a photograph of Evelyn, standing beside a man Ava recognized as the former school superintendent - the one who had mysteriously resigned last year amidst rumors of embezzlement. Their body language spoke volumes: heads close together, secretive smiles, hands clasped in what appeared to be more than a friendly gesture.

Ava's mind raced. Could this be the connection they'd been searching for? The leverage they needed?

"Find anything interesting?" Evelyn's voice, suddenly at her ear, made Ava jump.

She turned, meeting Evelyn's steel gaze with a forced calm she didn't feel. "Just appreciating your... photographic skills."

Evelyn's eyes narrowed dangerously. "Indeed. Perhaps we should continue this... survey... another time?"

As they were ushered out, Ava caught Johnson's knowing look. They'd struck gold, and Evelyn knew it. The hunt was on, and the predator had become the prey.

Outside, under the watchful gaze of Evelyn's mansion, Johnson pulled Ava close, his voice a low rumble. "We need to move fast. That photo could be our smoking gun."

Ava nodded, her mind already spinning with possibilities. "But how do we prove the connection without tipping our hand?"

Johnson's eyes gleamed with determination. "We dig deeper. Every secret leaves a trail, and Evelyn's just showed us where to start looking."

As they walked away, the weight of their discovery settled on Ava's shoulders. They were closer than ever to exposing Evelyn's true nature, but the path ahead was treacherous. One wrong move, and they could lose everything.

The game had changed, and the stakes had never been higher.

Ava's heart pounded as she and Johnson descended the mansion's steps, the weight of their discovery hanging heavy in the air. The photo burned in her mind, a sinister link between Evelyn and her past misdeeds.

"We're in this together now," Johnson murmured, his piercing blue eyes scanning the darkening street. "No turning back."

Ava nodded, her voice barely a whisper. "I wouldn't dream of it."

They paused at Johnson's car, a nondescript sedan that blended into the shadows. Ava's fingers trembled as she reached for the door handle, her mind racing with the implications of their alliance.

"You understand the risks?" Johnson asked, his weathered face etched with concern.

Ava met his gaze, her resolve hardening. "Evelyn's tormented me, threatened everything I hold dear. I'll do whatever it takes to stop her."

Johnson's lips quirked in a grim smile. "Then let's bring her down."

As they slid into the car, Ava felt a chill run down her spine. The road ahead was fraught with danger, but for the first time in months, she felt a flicker of hope.

The engine rumbled to life, and they pulled away from the curb. In the rearview mirror, Evelyn's mansion loomed like a malevolent specter, its windows gleaming with secrets yet to be uncovered.

Ava clenched her fists, steeling herself for the battle ahead. With Johnson by her side, they just might have a chance at exposing Evelyn's true nature and ending her reign of terror.

As they drove into the night, the air crackled with anticipation. The game was afoot, and Ava couldn't shake the feeling that their lives would never be the same again.

Chapter 7

The manila envelope sat on Ava's kitchen table like a ticking bomb. Her trembling fingers broke the seal, unleashing a flurry of legal jargon that made her head spin.

"This can't be happening," she whispered, scanning the documents with growing dread. John Summers' name glared up at her from the plaintiff line, accusing her of negligence and emotional distress.

Ava's chest constricted. The room seemed to darken, shadows creeping in from the corners. She stumbled to the sink, splashing cold water on her face.

"What did I do wrong?" Her reflection offered no answers, only hollow eyes staring back.

The ticking of the wall clock grew deafening. Tick. Tick. Tick. Each second another nail in the coffin of her reputation.

Ava slumped into a chair, her mind a maelstrom of doubt and fear. "I only wanted to help," she murmured. "How did it come to this?"

Memories flashed before her - Oliver's shy smile, Evelyn's venomous glare, John's calculating gaze. Had she misjudged everything? Was her kindness a fatal flaw?

The phone rang, shattering the silence. Ava flinched, letting it go to voicemail. She couldn't face anyone, not now. Not when her world was crumbling.

"What if they're right?" The thought slithered through her mind like a poisonous snake. "What if I am negligent?"

Ava's hands shook as she re-read the lawsuit. Each word seemed to accuse her, to strip away her carefully constructed identity. Who was she if not the devoted PTA president? If not the pillar of the community?

The walls of her cozy kitchen suddenly felt oppressive. Ava gasped for air, feeling trapped in a prison of her own making. How quickly the facade of normalcy could shatter, revealing the fragile nature of her existence.

As night fell, Ava remained frozen at the table, the legal documents her sole companion. The lawsuit loomed over her like a malevolent specter, whispering of ruin and disgrace. In the encroaching darkness, Ava Jennings faced her greatest fear - that perhaps, despite her best intentions, she had become the very thing she'd fought against all along.

The shadows lengthened as Ava's trembling fingers dialed Mrs. Thompson's number. Each ring echoed like a death knell in the stillness of her kitchen.

"Ava, dear?" Mrs. Thompson's warm voice filtered through, a lifeline in the darkness.

"I... I need help," Ava whispered, her words barely audible.

Mrs. Thompson's soothing tones washed over her. "Come over, child. The kettle's on."

Moments later, Ava found herself ensconced in Mrs. Thompson's floral-patterned armchair, a chipped teacup warming her hands. The room felt safe, a haven from the storm raging outside and within.

"You're stronger than you know, Ava," Mrs. Thompson murmured, her blue eyes gentle yet resolute. "This lawsuit... it's a test, not a sentence."

Ava's lip quivered. "But what if-"

"No," Mrs. Thompson interjected firmly. "You've poured your heart into this community. Don't let them tarnish that."

As Ava sipped her tea, a flicker of resolve kindled in her chest. Perhaps she wasn't alone after all.

The next morning, Ava's heels clicked ominously as she entered the police station. Detective Johnson's office loomed before her, a fortress of justice and hard truths.

"Ms. Jennings," he greeted, his piercing gaze softening slightly. "I heard about the lawsuit. Nasty business."

Ava nodded, her throat tight. "I... I don't know how to fight this."

Johnson leaned back, his chair creaking. "These types, they feed on fear. Don't give them the satisfaction."

"But how?" Ava asked, desperation seeping into her voice.

"Document everything," Johnson replied, his tone measured. "Every interaction, every alibi. And remember, the truth has a way of surfacing... even in the darkest waters."

As Ava left, Johnson's words echoed in her mind. The lawsuit still loomed, but now... now she had allies in this fight against the shadows.

The dim glow of Ava's laptop screen cast eerie shadows across her living room as she hunched over the keyboard, her fingers flying across the keys. The clock on the wall ticked relentlessly, a grim reminder of the impending legal battle.

"Frivolous lawsuits... precedents... defamation..." she muttered, her voice barely a whisper in the oppressive silence. Each new piece of information felt like a lifeline, yet simultaneously threatened to drag her deeper into the abyss of her fears.

Ava's eyes flicked to a framed photo of her students, their smiling faces a stark contrast to the darkness that seemed to seep into every corner of her home. *What if I lose everything?* The thought slithered through her mind, coiling around her heart.

She shook her head, banishing the treacherous thought. "No," she said aloud, her voice trembling but gaining strength. "I won't let them win."

The next morning, Ava found herself in her attorney's office, the air thick with tension and the faint scent of leather-bound law books.

"Ms. Jennings," her lawyer, a severe-looking woman named Ms. Blackwood, began, "I've reviewed the case. It's clear this is a vindictive attack, but we must tread carefully."

Ava nodded, her hands clasped tightly in her lap. "What's our strategy?"

Ms. Blackwood's lips curled into a thin smile that didn't reach her eyes. "We'll start by gathering character witnesses. Your reputation in the community will be our shield."

"And what about John Summers?" Ava asked, her voice barely above a whisper.

"Ah, Mr. Summers," Ms. Blackwood's tone dripped with disdain. "We'll expose his motivations. Every shadow has its source, Ms. Jennings. We just need to shine the right light."

As Ava left the office, a chill ran down her spine. The battle lines were drawn, but in this war of reputations, she couldn't shake the feeling that everyone would emerge with scars.

The courthouse loomed before Ava, a Gothic monstrosity of stone and shadow. She ascended the steps, each footfall echoing like a death knell in the oppressive silence. Inside, the air hung heavy with the weight of countless judgments passed.

Ava's breath caught as she spotted John Summers across the room. He stood tall, a shark in an expensive suit, exuding an aura of smug confidence that made her skin crawl. His eyes met hers, cold and calculating.

"All rise," the bailiff's voice cut through the tension.

As the judge entered, Ava's mind raced. *How did it come to this?* she wondered, her thoughts a desperate whisper in the stillness. *What sins am I atoning for?*

The proceedings droned on, a cacophony of legal jargon that seemed designed to obfuscate rather than illuminate. Ava's gaze kept drifting to John, who sat unnaturally still, a predator waiting to strike.

"Ms. Jennings," her attorney murmured, "stay focused. Don't let him intimidate you."

Ava nodded, but the words rang hollow. The courtroom walls seemed to close in, suffocating her with each passing moment.

Later, back at Pine View Elementary, Ava found solace in the unexpected warmth of her colleagues.

"We're behind you, Ava," Mrs. Thompson said, her wrinkled hand clasping Ava's. "This too shall pass."

The other teachers nodded in agreement, their faces etched with concern and support. Yet even as Ava felt buoyed by their faith, a nagging doubt lingered in the recesses of her mind.

Do they really believe in me, she wondered, *or is this just a performance of small-town solidarity?* The thought chilled her, a stark reminder that in this world of shadows and secrets, nothing was ever truly as it seemed.

The courthouse steps loomed before Ava, a stark monument to justice that now felt more like a harbinger of doom. As she descended, her heart pounding a staccato rhythm against her ribs, she caught sight of John Summers. He stood alone, a dark silhouette against the fading light.

Ava's feet carried her forward, each step echoing with newfound resolve. *This ends now*, she thought, her mind surprisingly clear.

"Mr. Summers," she called, her voice steady despite the tremor in her soul.

John turned, his face a mask of arrogant indifference. "Ms. Jennings. Come to beg for mercy?"

"No," Ava replied, meeting his gaze unflinchingly. "I've come to tell you that your intimidation tactics won't work. I am innocent, and I will not be cowed by your threats or your wealth."

A flicker of surprise crossed John's features before his lips curled into a sneer. "Bold words from a woman facing ruin."

"Perhaps," Ava conceded, her voice low and haunting. "But I'd rather face ruin with my integrity intact than live as a coward hiding behind frivolous lawsuits."

John's eyes narrowed dangerously. "You have no idea what you're up against."

"Neither do you," Ava retorted, turning away. As she walked into the encroaching darkness, she felt John's gaze boring into her back, a silent promise of retribution.

The following day, Ava threw herself into her work at Pine View Elementary with renewed vigor. As she hung colorful posters for the upcoming science fair, she couldn't shake the feeling of being watched.

"Mrs. Jennings?" a small voice piped up. Oliver Summers stood before her, his innocent eyes wide with curiosity.

Ava's heart clenched. "Yes, Oliver?"

"Are you okay? You look sad."

Forcing a smile, Ava knelt to his level. "I'm fine, sweetheart. Just a bit tired. Are you excited for the science fair?"

As Oliver chattered about his project, Ava's mind wandered. *How can I protect these children from the darkness that surrounds us?* she mused, the weight of her responsibility settling heavily on her shoulders.

The day wore on, a blur of meetings and preparations. As twilight fell, Ava found herself alone in her office, the shadows lengthening ominously around her.

What fresh horror awaits me tomorrow? she wondered, her fingers tracing the edge of a legal document. *And how long can I keep fighting before the darkness consumes me entirely?*

The courtroom loomed, a cathedral of justice bathed in sickly fluorescent light. Ava's heart thundered as she took her seat, the wooden bench creaking ominously beneath her. Her attorney, a gaunt figure in a charcoal suit, leaned close, his whisper a ghostly caress.

"We have them, Ava. The evidence..." His words trailed off, swallowed by the oppressive silence.

John Summers sat across the aisle, his face an alabaster mask of confidence. But Ava saw the flicker of uncertainty in his eyes, a crack in his impenetrable facade.

The judge, a specter draped in black robes, called the court to order. Ava's attorney rose, his movements fluid yet somehow disjointed.

"Your Honor, I present Exhibit A," he intoned, his voice echoing in the cavernous room. "Security footage from Pine View Elementary on the day in question."

As the grainy video played, Ava's breath caught in her throat. There, clear as day, was John Summers, planting evidence in her office.

How did we miss this? Ava wondered, her mind reeling. *And what darkness drove him to such depths?*

The judge leaned forward, his weathered face a landscape of deep furrows. "Mr. Summers, would you care to explain?"

John's composure crumbled, his mask slipping to reveal the tormented soul beneath. "I... I had no choice," he stammered, his words heavy with the weight of his sins.

As the gavel fell, dismissing the case, Ava felt a great burden lift. Yet, a lingering unease remained, whispering of battles yet to come.

"It's over," her attorney murmured, but Ava knew better. In Oakwood, nothing truly ended; it merely transformed, taking on new, more insidious forms.

Ava stood at the window of her dimly lit living room, her reflection ghostly in the rain-streaked glass. The courtroom victory felt hollow, a pyrrhic triumph that left her soul weary.

"I should feel elated," she whispered to the empty room, her words barely audible over the patter of raindrops. "So why does this dread linger?"

She turned, her eyes falling on the scattered letters of support from her allies - Mrs. Thompson, Detective Johnson, her colleagues at Pine View. Each one a lifeline in the storm she'd weathered.

I've changed, Ava realized, tracing the contours of her face in the window. *The Ava they knew is gone.*

The phone rang, shattering the silence. Ava hesitated, her hand hovering over the receiver.

"Hello?" she answered, her voice steady despite the tremor in her heart.

"It's not over, Ava," Evelyn's voice slithered through the line, dripping with venom. "John may have faltered, but I won't rest until—"

Ava hung up, her jaw set. "No," she said to the dial tone. "You won't."

She moved to her desk, pulling out a notebook. As she began to write, plans forming on the page, a small smile played at her lips.

Let them come, she thought, her pen scratching across the paper. I'm ready now.

Outside, the storm intensified, mirroring the tempest brewing in Oakwood's quiet streets. Ava worked late into the night, preparing for the battle to come, unaware of the dark forces already aligning against her.

Chapter 8

Ava's sensible flats clicked against the cracked pavement as she approached Pine View Elementary. The morning air hung heavy, weighted with unspoken accusations. A cluster of parents huddled near the entrance, their whispers slithering through the fog like serpents.

Mrs. Thompson's eyes narrowed as Ava passed. "Morning," Ava offered with a strained smile. Silence swallowed her greeting whole.

They know. Somehow, they all know.

Ava's heart hammered against her ribs as she pushed open the school's ancient oak doors. The familiar scent of chalk dust and floor wax did nothing to calm her nerves.

In the teacher's lounge, conversation died as she entered. Her colleagues averted their gazes, suddenly fascinated by the dregs in their coffee mugs.

"Did you hear what Evelyn's been saying?" Ms. Garcia's hushed voice carried from the corner. "About Ava and that incident with Oliver?"

Mr. Peterson shook his head. "John's got the school board involved now. Says Ava's unfit—"

Their words faded as blood rushed in Ava's ears. She gripped the edge of the counter, knuckles white.

Breathe. Just breathe.

"Morning, everyone," Ava managed, her voice steadier than she felt. "Looks like it might rain later."

A few mumbled responses. Ms. Garcia's cheeks flushed as she busied herself with stirring her coffee.

Ava poured herself a cup, the bitter liquid scalding her tongue. "I was thinking we could finalize plans for the spring fair today. Any volunteers?"

Silence stretched, taut as a bowstring.

They're afraid. Afraid of me. Of what associating with me might mean.

"I'll help," Mr. Peterson offered quietly, not quite meeting her eyes.

Ava nodded, gratitude and despair warring within her chest. "Thank you, Tom. We'll chat after lunch?"

As she left the lounge, the whispers resumed. Ava's shoulders slumped beneath the weight of unspoken judgments. The hallway before her seemed to elongate, a gauntlet she must run each day.

How long can I endure this? How long before they break me?

Ava squared her shoulders, lifting her chin. She would not give Evelyn and John the satisfaction. Not today. Not ever.

The fluorescent lights flickered ominously as Ava made her way down the corridor, casting grotesque shadows that seemed to reach for her with gnarled fingers. The once-familiar hallway now felt like a twisted funhouse mirror, distorting everything she thought she knew.

A sharp rap on the window of Principal Davis's office made her jump. He beckoned her inside, his usually warm smile now a thin, strained line. As Ava entered, the door clicked shut behind her with an air of finality.

"Ava," Principal Davis began, his voice low and grave. "I'm afraid we have a situation."

She sank into the chair across from him, her heart a leaden weight in her chest. "The complaints," she whispered, more to herself than to him.

He nodded, removing his glasses to pinch the bridge of his nose. "Parents are... concerned. The board is breathing down my neck. I'm under immense pressure to address this."

Ava's mind raced, memories of past triumphs and failures swirling in a dizzying maelstrom. *How quickly they turn,* she thought bitterly. *All those years of dedication, reduced to ashes by a whisper campaign.*

"Principal Davis," she began, her voice surprisingly steady, "I understand the gravity of the situation. But I assure you, these accusations are baseless."

She reached into her bag, withdrawing a folder. "I've compiled evidence—character references, time-stamped photos, even security footage—that disproves every allegation made against me."

As she spoke, laying out her case with meticulous care, Ava felt a glimmer of hope. Surely, faced with the truth, reason would prevail. Yet a nagging voice whispered in the back of her mind: *In a world of smoke and mirrors, does truth even matter anymore?*

Principal Davis listened intently, his brow furrowed in concentration. When Ava finished, he let out a long, weary sigh. "Ava, I want to believe you. I do. But—"

"But what?" Ava interrupted, a hint of steel creeping into her tone. "Isn't the truth enough?"

The silence that followed was deafening, filled with unspoken truths and the ghosts of shattered trust.

Principal Davis leaned back in his chair, the leather creaking ominously in the oppressive silence. His eyes, usually warm and understanding, now held a glacial coolness that sent a chill down Ava's spine.

"The truth, Ava," he said softly, each word falling like a leaden weight, "is not always enough in the court of public opinion. The damage to the school's reputation... it's substantial."

Ava felt the walls of the office closing in, suffocating her with their indifference. She clenched her fists, nails biting into her palms, anchoring her to reality.

"I think," Principal Davis continued, his voice a funeral dirge, "it would be best if you took a temporary leave of absence. Just until this... situation... resolves itself."

The words hung in the air like a guillotine blade, poised to sever Ava's last lifeline to normalcy. She closed her eyes, memories of laughing children and grateful parents flashing behind her eyelids. *No,* she thought fiercely. *I will not be cast out like a pariah.*

"With all due respect, Principal Davis," Ava said, her voice low and intense, "I cannot – will not – abandon these children. My work here is too important."

She leaned forward, her eyes blazing with a fervent light. "This community has been my home, my purpose. I've poured my heart and soul into these halls. To leave now would be to admit defeat, to let Evelyn and John's vindictiveness win."

Principal Davis shifted uncomfortably, avoiding her gaze. "Ava, please understand—"

"No," she interrupted, her voice trembling with emotion. "You understand. I will continue my work here, come hell or high water. These children need me, and I need them."

The clock on the wall ticked relentlessly, marking the passing of seconds that felt like eternities. In that moment, Ava knew she stood at a crossroads, her fate balanced on a knife's edge.

As Ava left Principal Davis's office, the hallway seemed to stretch endlessly before her, a gauntlet of whispers and sidelong glances. She held her head high, but each step felt like wading through molasses, the weight of unseen eyes pressing down upon her.

A cluster of parents huddled near the water fountain, their conversation dying as Ava approached. One mother – Sarah, whose daughter Ava had tutored last spring – averted her gaze, suddenly fascinated by the linoleum floor.

Is this how quickly loyalties crumble? Ava wondered, her heart constricting.

"Good morning," she offered, her voice steady despite the tremor in her soul.

Silence greeted her. Then, a murmured "morning" from the group's periphery, grudging as a child forced to apologize.

Ava pressed on, each step an act of defiance against the growing void around her. She reached the teacher's lounge, seeking solace in familiar faces.

But as she pushed open the door, conversations hushed. Her colleagues – friends, she'd thought – found sudden interest in their coffee cups or smartphones.

"Hey, everyone," Ava said, injecting cheer she didn't feel into her voice. "Quite a morning, huh?"

Mark, the third-grade teacher who'd always had a kind word, mumbled something unintelligible and hurried past her.

Even you? The betrayal stung like salt in an open wound.

Ava stood alone in the center of the room, an island in a sea of averted gazes and uncomfortable silence. The clock ticked, each second an eternity of isolation.

The shrill ring of Ava's phone sliced through the suffocating silence, startling her from her reverie. Her trembling fingers fumbled with the device, nearly dropping it as she retreated to a secluded corner of the lounge.

"Hello?" she whispered, her voice hoarse with unspoken anguish.

"Ms. Jennings, it's Detective Johnson." The gruff voice on the other end sent a shiver down her spine. "We need to talk. Now."

Ava's heart quickened, a caged bird thrashing against her ribs. "What is it? Have you—"

"Not over the phone," he interrupted, his tone low and urgent. "Meet me at Blackwood Park in fifteen minutes. Come alone."

The line went dead, leaving Ava with a growing sense of dread. She glanced at her colleagues, still studiously ignoring her presence. *Would they even notice if I vanished?* she wondered bitterly.

Slipping out of the school felt like escaping a prison, the weight of judgment lifting momentarily as she stepped into the crisp autumn air. Fallen leaves crunched beneath her feet as she hurried towards Blackwood Park, its gnarled trees looming like ancient sentinels.

Detective Johnson materialized from behind a weathered oak, his face grave. "Ms. Jennings," he nodded, gesturing for her to follow him deeper into the park's shadowy recesses.

"What's going on?" Ava asked, her voice barely above a whisper.

The detective's eyes darted around before he spoke. "We've got them, Ava. Surveillance footage from the Oakwood Inn. John Summers, clear as day, making that 'anonymous' call."

Ava's breath caught in her throat. "You mean—"

"It's the break we needed," Johnson confirmed, a grim smile tugging at his lips. "But tread carefully. Cornered rats are the most dangerous kind."

Ava's mind reeled, hope and fear warring within her. The detective's piercing blue eyes bore into her, his weathered face etched with concern.

"We're building a strong case," Johnson continued, his voice a low rumble. "But the Summers... they're not to be underestimated. Wealth, connections, a ruthless determination to protect their own."

A chill wind rustled through the dying leaves, carrying with it the scent of decay. Ava shivered, wrapping her arms around herself. "What do you mean?"

Johnson's gaze darted around the park, as if expecting shadows to come alive. "People like them, they don't play by the rules. They'll do anything to keep their reputation intact. Anything."

The unspoken threat hung in the air between them, as tangible as the mist curling around their feet. Ava's throat constricted, memories of whispered accusations and judgmental stares flashing through her mind.

"So what do we do?" she asked, hating how small her voice sounded.

The detective's hand rested briefly on her shoulder, a fleeting comfort. "We keep pushing, but smart. Cautious. You need to watch your back, Ava. Every step, every word."

Ava nodded, a spark of defiance igniting in her chest. "I won't let them win," she declared, her voice steadier now. "Not after everything they've done."

Johnson's lips quirked in a half-smile. "That's the spirit. Just... be careful. These people, they're like poison. Insidious."

"Thank you," Ava said softly, genuine gratitude warming her words. "For believing in me, for fighting this fight."

The detective nodded solemnly. "Justice is worth fighting for. No matter the cost."

As they parted ways, Ava couldn't shake the feeling that she was being watched, unseen eyes boring into her back. The park seemed to close in around her, its beauty twisting into something sinister. But beneath the fear, a newfound resolve burned bright. She would see this through, come what may.

The hallway stretched before Ava like a gauntlet, shadows lengthening as the day waned. Her footsteps echoed, a lonely rhythm against whispered judgments that seemed to seep from the very walls. At the far end, a figure materialized - Evelyn, her perfectly coiffed hair and designer outfit a stark contrast to the dimness surrounding her.

"Well, well," Evelyn's voice dripped with saccharine malice. "If it isn't our dear, beleaguered volunteer."

Ava's heart thundered, but she steadied herself. "Evelyn," she acknowledged, her tone carefully neutral.

Evelyn's lips curled into a predatory smile. "Still clinging to your... position here? How... admirable."

"I have nothing to hide," Ava countered, her voice low but firm. "Your lies won't change that."

A flicker of something - anger? fear? - flashed in Evelyn's eyes. "Lies? Oh, darling. You have no idea what truths are lurking in the shadows, do you?"

Ava's mind raced, Detective Johnson's warnings echoing. She chose her next words carefully. "Whatever game you're playing, Evelyn, it won't work. The truth always comes out."

Evelyn leaned in, her perfume cloying. "Does it now? And what price are you willing to pay for your... truth?"

A chill slithered down Ava's spine, but she held Evelyn's gaze. "Whatever it takes."

As Evelyn sauntered away, her laughter trailing like poison, Ava sagged against the wall, exhaling shakily. The encounter left her drained, doubt gnawing at the edges of her resolve.

Later, as twilight painted the sky in bruised hues, Ava gathered her things. The day's weight pressed upon her, each whisper and sidelong glance another stone added to her burden. Yet as she neared the exit, a small group awaited her - Ms. Patel, the art teacher, and Mr. Guzman from the science department.

"Ava," Ms. Patel's warm voice wrapped around her like a balm. "We just wanted you to know... we're with you."

Mr. Guzman nodded solemnly. "This witch hunt... it isn't right. We've got your back."

Tears pricked at Ava's eyes, a lump forming in her throat. "Thank you," she managed, the simple words inadequate for the surge of gratitude she felt.

As they parted ways, Ava's steps felt lighter. The road ahead was treacherous, fraught with unseen perils, but she was not alone. In the gathering gloom, a flicker of hope persisted, fragile but unextinguished.

Ava stepped into the evening, the school's shadow stretching long and dark across the empty playground. A chill wind whispered through bare branches, carrying echoes of childish laughter now turned to silence. She paused, her hand lingering on the cool metal of the gate.

"You won't break me," she murmured, her words lost to the encroaching night. Her eyes, once soft with kindness, now glinted with steely determination.

As she walked to her car, the click of her heels on pavement rang out like a battle cry. Each step forward was a rejection of retreat, a defiance of the whispers that sought to drive her away.

Ava's mind raced, plotting her next move. "Evelyn and John think they have the upper hand," she thought, a wry smile tugging at her lips. "But they don't know what I'm capable of."

Reaching her vehicle, she noticed a folded note tucked beneath the windshield wiper. Her heart quickened as she unfolded it, revealing a message in an unfamiliar scrawl:

"Watch your back. Not everyone is who they seem."

Ava's laugh was hollow, tinged with bitterness. "Oh, Evelyn," she said aloud, crumpling the paper. "You'll have to do better than that."

As she slid into the driver's seat, her phone buzzed. Detective Johnson's name flashed on the screen.

"Any news?" Ava answered, her voice low and urgent.

"We're close," came the detective's gravelly reply. "But be careful. These people... they're dangerous."

Ava's grip tightened on the steering wheel. "I know," she said, her tone matching the darkness gathering around her. "But so am I."

Chapter 9

The radio crackled to life, its static-laced voice cutting through the stale air of the patrol car. Officer Daniels leaned in, his weathered face tightening as he listened to the dispatcher's urgent tone.

"We've got an anonymous tip about a potential DUI. Female driver, erratic behavior. Suspect identified as Ava Jennings, currently at Pine View Elementary."

Daniels exchanged a glance with his partner, Officer Chen. The name hung in the air like a funeral dirge.

"Ava Jennings? The PTA president?" Chen's voice dripped with disbelief.

Daniels nodded, his eyes darkening. "Sometimes the most respectable facades hide the darkest secrets."

They peeled out of the parking lot, sirens wailing a mournful cry. The school loomed ahead, its cheerful exterior a stark contrast to the dread pooling in Daniels' gut.

"I've seen her at community events," Chen mused, his fingers drumming an anxious rhythm on the dashboard. "Always so put-together, so... perfect."

Daniels' laugh was hollow. "Perfect's just another word for 'good at hiding things.'"

As they pulled into the school parking lot, Daniels couldn't shake the feeling that they were about to unearth something sinister. The playground equipment cast long shadows, like grasping fingers reaching for unsuspecting victims.

"Let's do this by the book," Daniels muttered, more to himself than to Chen. "No matter who she is, if she's putting kids at risk..."

He left the sentence unfinished, the unspoken consequences hanging in the air like a executioner's axe.

Ava's lilting voice carried through the art room as she helped a group of third-graders with their papier-mâché projects. Her hands, stained with flecks of paint and glue, moved deftly as she molded newspaper strips into fantastical shapes.

"Remember, Julia," she said softly to a freckled girl with pigtails, "art isn't about perfection. It's about expressing what's inside you."

The child beamed, her earlier frustration melting away. Ava's heart swelled, momentarily pushing back the shadows that had been haunting her thoughts. This was why she volunteered—to make a difference, however small.

A commotion in the hallway drew her attention. Curious whispers rippled through the classroom like a dark tide.

"Is that... the police?" Mrs. Holloway, the art teacher, peered through the doorway, her face pale.

Ava's stomach clenched, an irrational fear gripping her. "I'm sure it's nothing," she reassured, her voice steadier than she felt. "Probably just a routine visit."

But as she turned back to the children, she caught sight of Officer Daniels' grim expression through the classroom window. His eyes locked with hers, and in that moment, Ava knew. The carefully constructed facade of her life was about to shatter.

"Mrs. Jennings?" he called, his voice carrying an undercurrent of authority that sent chills down her spine. "We need to speak with you."

The children's eyes widened, a mix of excitement and apprehension on their faces. Ava forced a smile, her heart thundering in her chest.

"Of course, officer," she replied, her mind racing. What could they want? What had she done?

As she walked towards the door, Julia's small voice piped up, "Are you in trouble, Mrs. Jennings?"

Ava paused, her hand on the doorknob. "No, sweetie," she lied, the words tasting like ashes in her mouth. "Everything's fine."

But as she stepped into the hallway, the weight of unspoken accusations pressing down on her, Ava knew that nothing would ever be fine again.

Ava's footsteps echoed in the hallway, each click of her sensible heels a drumbeat of dread. She approached the officers, her smile a brittle mask that threatened to crack at any moment.

"Officers," she greeted, her voice honey-sweet but laced with an undercurrent of fear. "How can I help you today?"

Officer Daniels cleared his throat, his eyes darting to the curious faces pressed against the classroom windows. "Mrs. Jennings, we've received an anonymous tip about your... behavior. They claim you've been driving erratically, possibly under the influence."

The words hit Ava like a physical blow. She stumbled, catching herself against the wall, her mind reeling. "I... what? That's absurd," she whispered, her carefully cultivated composure crumbling.

"We need to search your vehicle," his partner, Officer Rivera, interjected. "For any signs of illegal substances."

Ava's world tilted on its axis. The fluorescent lights overhead seemed to flicker, casting grotesque shadows across the officers' faces. She could feel the weight of dozens of eyes upon her, judging, condemning.

"This is a mistake," she pleaded, her voice barely audible. "I would never... the children..."

But even as she spoke, a treacherous voice in the back of her mind whispered, *What if you did? What if you've forgotten?* The thought sent a chill down her spine, a creeping horror that threatened to consume her.

With trembling fingers, Ava reached into her pocket and produced her car keys. The metal felt unnaturally cold against her skin, as if infused with the icy dread that now coursed through her veins. She held them out to Officer Daniels, her hand shaking so violently that the keys jangled like macabre wind chimes.

"Here," she whispered, her voice a brittle thread. "But I assure you, there's nothing to find."

As the officers moved towards her modest sedan, Ava became acutely aware of the growing crowd. Faces pressed against windows, bodies huddled in doorways, whispers slithering through the air like poison. She could feel their eyes boring into her, peeling away layers of respectability she'd so carefully constructed over the years.

How did it come to this? The thought echoed in her mind, a haunting refrain. She watched, helpless, as Officer Rivera popped open her trunk, methodically rifling through the detritus of her everyday life. Each item examined felt like another indignity, another violation.

"Mrs. Jennings?" A small voice pierced her spiraling thoughts. It was Timmy, a second-grader with perpetually untied shoelaces. "Are you in trouble?"

Ava's heart clenched. She forced a smile, though it felt more like a grimace. "No, sweetheart. It's just a misunderstanding."

But even as the words left her lips, doubt gnawed at her. Who would do this to her? Who hated her enough to fabricate such a damning accusation? The possibilities swirled in her mind, each more terrifying than the last. Old rivalries, perceived slights, hidden resentments – they all rose up like specters, taunting her with their malevolent grins.

Officer Martinez's voice cut through Ava's reverie, sharp and ominous. "What's this?"

Ava turned, her heart plummeting as she saw the officer's gloved hand disappear beneath the upholstery of her car's trunk. A hidden compartment. How? When? Her mind reeled.

"I... I don't understand," Ava stammered, her usual composure crumbling. "That's not possible."

The officer emerged, holding a small package wrapped in dark plastic. The world seemed to tilt on its axis as he carefully peeled back the layers, revealing a white, powdery substance.

Gasps rippled through the crowd. Ava felt the weight of their judgment crushing her, each whisper a dagger to her carefully cultivated reputation.

"Oh my God," Mrs. Thompson, a fellow volunteer, muttered. "I never would have thought..."

"But she seemed so nice," a student's voice piped up, laced with confusion and betrayal.

Ava's cheeks burned with shame, her throat constricting. "This is a mistake," she choked out, her voice barely above a whisper. "I've never seen that before in my life."

Officer Rivera's eyes met hers, a mix of pity and suspicion. "Ma'am, we're going to need you to come with us."

The world blurred around Ava, faces melting into a sea of accusation and disbelief. How had her life unraveled so completely in the span of mere minutes? The grounds of Pine View Elementary, once her sanctuary, now felt like a nightmare from which she couldn't wake.

Ava's heart thundered in her chest, but she forced her face into a mask of calm. Years of PTA meetings and school crises had honed her ability to maintain composure, even as her world crumbled around her.

"Of course, Officer," she said, her voice steady despite the tremor in her hands. "I'll cooperate fully."

As the officers finished their search, Ava's mind whirled like a dervish. Who could have planted those drugs? Who would want to destroy her like this? The faces of colleagues, parents, even students flashed before her eyes, each a potential betrayer.

Officer Rivera approached, his expression grave. "Mrs. Jennings, we'll need you to come down to the station for questioning."

Ava nodded, swallowing hard. "I understand. May I... may I have a moment to speak with Principal Hawthorne?"

The officer hesitated, then nodded. Ava turned to face her longtime friend and colleague, whose face was a mask of shock and disappointment.

"Sarah," Ava began, her voice low and urgent, "I swear to you, I had no idea about any of this. Someone's set me up."

Principal Hawthorne's eyes softened slightly. "Ava, I... I want to believe you. But this looks bad. Really bad."

Ava felt a flicker of resolve ignite within her. "I know. But I will get to the bottom of this. I have to."

As she was led to the police car, Ava's mind raced. She would prove her innocence. She would uncover the truth. And heaven help whoever had done this to her, for they had no idea of the storm they had unleashed.

The police cruiser's door slammed shut with a finality that echoed through Ava's bones. As they pulled away from Pine View Elementary, she caught glimpses of familiar faces—colleagues, parents, students—all wearing expressions of shock, disbelief, and judgment. Their eyes bored into her, each gaze a dagger to her carefully crafted reputation.

"This can't be happening," Ava whispered, her voice barely audible over the cruiser's engine.

Officer Rivera glanced at her in the rearview mirror. "Ma'am, anything you say can be used—"

"I know my rights," Ava interrupted, her usual warmth replaced by a chill that surprised even her. She turned to look out the window, watching as her beloved community receded into the distance.

The rhythmic thrum of tires on asphalt became a haunting metronome, marking the seconds of her descent into this nightmare. Ava's mind raced, conjuring images of newspaper headlines, whispered conversations at PTA meetings, and the disappointed faces of the children she'd worked so hard to support.

As they drove, shadows seemed to lengthen, stretching across the familiar streets of Oakwood like grasping fingers. Ava shuddered, feeling as though the very town was turning against her, eager to swallow her whole.

"Who could have done this?" she thought, her inner voice trembling. "And why? What sin from my past has come to haunt me?"

The police station loomed ahead, a monolithic structure that seemed to pulse with malevolent intent. As they approached, Ava steeled herself, determined to face whatever horrors awaited her within those walls.

But even as she summoned her courage, a creeping dread wormed its way into her heart, whispering that perhaps this was only the beginning of her torment.

Chapter 10

The steering wheel creaked under Ava's white-knuckled grip as shadows lengthened across the elementary school parking lot. A chill wind whispered through barren branches, echoing the hollow ache in her chest. How had it come to this - her sanctuary become a battleground, her passion twisted into something sinister?

Ava's eyes darted to the rearview mirror, searching for phantoms. Was that Evelyn's accusatory glare lurking behind every window pane? The imagined weight of judging stares pressed down, squeezing the air from her lungs.

"I've done nothing wrong," she whispered, the words tasting of ash. But doubt gnawed at the edges of her conviction. Had she been blind to some grave misstep, some fatal flaw that now threatened to unravel everything she'd built?

A gentle tap at the window startled Ava from her spiral. Mrs. Thompson's concerned face swam into focus through the glass, her hand raised in a tentative wave. The older woman's presence was at once comforting and terrifying. Did she too harbor suspicions?

"Ava, dear? Are you alright?" Mrs. Thompson's muffled voice carried a note of worry.

Ava forced a brittle smile, her mask slipping into place with practiced ease. "Of course, just... lost in thought." The lie slithered past her lips, leaving a bitter aftertaste.

Mrs. Thompson's brow furrowed, seeing through the facade. She motioned for Ava to roll down the window, her expression a mixture of concern and determination.

As Ava's finger hovered over the switch, paranoia whispered its poison. What if this was a trap? What if Mrs. Thompson was here to confront her, to add her voice to the growing chorus of accusation?

The silence stretched, charged with unspoken tension. In that moment, Ava teetered on a precipice, one choice away from either salvation or damnation.

With trembling fingers, Ava pressed the button. The window descended, letting in a gust of cool air that carried the faint scent of Mrs. Thompson's lavender perfume. It was a scent that had once brought comfort, but now it seemed to wrap around Ava's throat like a noose.

"My dear," Mrs. Thompson's voice was a gentle caress, "you look as though you're carrying the weight of the world on your shoulders."

Ava's laugh was a brittle thing, sharp enough to cut. "Oh, you know how it is. PTA duties never end."

Mrs. Thompson's eyes, warm and knowing, bore into Ava's soul. "I think perhaps we both know there's more to it than that. Why don't you step out for a moment? A walk might do you good."

The invitation hung in the air, laden with unspoken understanding. Ava's mind raced. Was this an olive branch or a summons to her own execution?

"I... I'm not sure that's a good idea," Ava whispered, her voice barely audible over the pounding of her heart.

Mrs. Thompson's smile was tinged with sadness. "Sometimes, Ava, the things we're most afraid of are the very things we need to face."

The words struck Ava like a physical blow. How much did Mrs. Thompson know? How much had she guessed?

Ava's fingers trembled as she grasped the door handle, the cool metal a stark contrast to her feverish skin. With a deep, shuddering breath that seemed to rattle the very core of her being, she stepped out into the crisp autumn air.

Mrs. Thompson's presence loomed beside her, a specter of comfort and dread intertwined. They began to walk, their footsteps crunching softly on the gravel path that snaked through the school grounds like a sinister serpent.

"I... I don't know where to begin," Ava confessed, her voice barely above a whisper. The words felt heavy on her tongue, laden with secrets she'd kept buried for far too long.

Mrs. Thompson's hand ghosted over Ava's arm, a touch so light it might have been imagined. "The beginning is often a good place, my dear. But sometimes, it's the middle where the true story lies."

Ava's laugh was a hollow thing, echoing in the emptiness between them. "The middle? Oh, Mrs. Thompson, I fear I'm nearing the end."

As they walked, Ava's fears and doubts poured forth like a noxious flood. "Evelyn's accusations... they're not entirely baseless. There are things in my past, things I've done..."

Mrs. Thompson listened, her face a mask of empathy that Ava couldn't quite trust. Was that a flicker of judgment in those kind eyes? A shadow of disgust?

"We all have our demons, Ava," Mrs. Thompson murmured. "It's how we face them that defines us."

Ava's mind reeled. Could she truly confess the depths of her transgressions? The weight of her secrets threatened to crush her, even as Mrs. Thompson's words offered a lifeline she wasn't sure she deserved.

The gnarled oak loomed before them, its twisted branches reaching out like grasping fingers. Beneath its ominous canopy sat a weathered bench, beckoning them with deceptive promise of respite.

Ava collapsed onto the seat, her composure finally shattering. Sobs wracked her body, each gasp tearing from her throat like a confession.

"I can't... I can't do this anymore," she choked out between ragged breaths. The facade of the perfect PTA president crumbled, revealing the tormented soul beneath.

Mrs. Thompson settled beside her, a warm presence in the chill of Ava's despair. "Oh, Ava," she murmured, her voice a soothing balm that only served to heighten Ava's anguish.

"You don't understand," Ava whispered, her words barely audible. "The things I've done to protect my position, to maintain this illusion of perfection..."

Mrs. Thompson's hand found Ava's shoulder, the touch both comforting and terrifying. "We all have our shadows, dear. But you possess a strength that few can match."

Ava's laugh was bitter, tainted with self-loathing. "Strength? I'm a fraud, Mrs. Thompson. A liar and a cheat."

"Perhaps," Mrs. Thompson conceded, her words hanging in the air like a guillotine's blade. "But you're also a fighter, Ava. You've always been true to your core, even when the path was shrouded in darkness."

Ava's mind reeled. Could redemption truly be possible? Or was Mrs. Thompson's kindness just another manipulation, another layer of deceit in this web of lies?

A shiver crawled up Ava's spine as Mrs. Thompson's words sank in. The gnarled oak above them creaked ominously, its shadows dancing across the ground like restless spirits.

"True to my core?" Ava echoed, her voice hollow. "I'm not sure I even know what that is anymore."

Mrs. Thompson's eyes glinted with an unnerving wisdom. "Oh, but you do, dear. It's buried deep, beneath the layers of guilt and fear."

Ava's hands trembled as she wiped away her tears. "How can you be so certain?"

"Because I've seen it," Mrs. Thompson replied, her tone suddenly sharp. "I've watched you fight for these children, even when the cost was your own peace of mind."

A memory flashed through Ava's mind – Evelyn's accusatory glare, the weight of unspoken threats. She swallowed hard, steeling herself.

"You're right," Ava whispered, more to herself than to Mrs. Thompson. "I can't let Evelyn win. Not when there's so much at stake."

They rose from the bench, the air around them thick with unspoken truths. As they continued their walk, Ava's steps grew more purposeful, her chin lifting ever so slightly.

"What if I'm not strong enough?" Ava murmured, the doubt still clinging to her like a second skin.

Mrs. Thompson's laugh was soft, almost musical. "My dear, you've always been stronger than you know. The question is, are you ready to embrace that strength?"

Ava nodded, a grim smile playing at her lips. "I have to be. For the children. For myself."

The school loomed ahead, a fortress of secrets and whispered accusations. Ava squared her shoulders, ready to face whatever darkness lay within.

As they rounded the corner of the school building, a figure materialized from the shadows. Principal Davis stood like a sentinel, his salt-and-pepper hair catching the wan light. Ava's breath caught in her throat. Was this an omen or an opportunity?

"Now's your chance," Mrs. Thompson whispered, her voice carrying a hint of urgency that sent chills down Ava's spine.

Ava nodded, her heart pounding a frantic rhythm against her ribs. She approached Principal Davis, each step feeling like a march towards judgment.

"Principal Davis," Ava called out, her voice steadier than she felt. "Might I have a word?"

He turned, his bespectacled gaze landing on Ava with an intensity that made her want to shrink away. But she held her ground, feeling Mrs. Thompson's steadying presence behind her.

"Mrs. Jennings," Principal Davis replied, his tone carefully neutral. "I was hoping we'd have a chance to talk."

Ava's mind raced. What did he know? What whispers had reached his ears? She forced a smile, praying it didn't look as brittle as it felt.

"I believe we have much to discuss," Ava said, the words tasting like ash in her mouth. She glanced at Mrs. Thompson, drawing strength from her encouraging nod.

Principal Davis's expression softened, concern etching lines around his eyes. "Indeed we do. Shall we step into my office?"

As they walked towards the building, Ava couldn't shake the feeling that she was walking into the lion's den. But there was no turning back now. The truth, no matter how painful, had to be faced.

Ava's fingers trembled as she clasped them tightly in her lap, the weight of her impending confession pressing down upon her like a shroud. Principal Davis's office seemed to close in around her, the walls whispering accusations she couldn't quite hear.

"Evelyn Summers," Ava began, her voice barely above a whisper, "she's been... relentless." The word hung in the air, heavy with unspoken horrors.

Principal Davis leaned forward, his salt-and-pepper brows furrowing. "Go on," he urged gently.

Ava took a shuddering breath. "She's accusing me of favoritism, of neglecting her son Oliver. But it's not true." Her voice cracked, memories of Evelyn's venomous words slithering through her mind. "I've only ever wanted what's best for all the children."

As she spoke, Ava's gaze darted around the room, half-expecting to see Evelyn's malevolent shadow lurking in the corners. Principal Davis listened intently, his expression growing increasingly grave.

"I fear," Ava continued, her words now tumbling out in a desperate rush, "that she won't stop until she's destroyed everything I've worked for. The PTA, my reputation, my..." She trailed off, unable to voice her deepest fear - losing the children she'd come to love as her own.

Principal Davis's silence stretched on, each passing second feeling like an eternity of judgment. Ava's heart pounded in her ears, a dreadful countdown to her inevitable downfall.

Principal Davis's chair creaked ominously as he leaned back, his eyes piercing through Ava like spectral daggers. The room seemed to darken, shadows creeping along the edges of her vision.

"Mrs. Jennings," he began, his voice low and measured, "I want you to know that your dedication to this school has not gone unnoticed."

Ava's breath caught in her throat, a flicker of hope igniting in her chest. Could it be?

"Rest assured," Principal Davis continued, his words carrying the weight of a solemn oath, "I will do everything in my power to support you and ensure justice is served."

Relief washed over Ava, but it was tinged with a lingering dread. She'd heard promises before, seen them dissipate like morning mist.

"What... what will you do?" she asked, her voice trembling.

Principal Davis's eyes glinted with determination. "I'll be taking immediate action to address Mrs. Summers' behavior. Her accusations will not go unchallenged."

As he spoke, Ava couldn't shake the feeling that unseen forces were at play. Would this truly be her salvation, or merely the calm before an even greater storm?

"Thank you," she whispered, the words tasting both sweet and bitter on her tongue.

As she left the office, Ava felt a chill run down her spine. The hallway stretched before her, long and dark, echoing with the ghosts of past transgressions and the whispers of battles yet to come.

Chapter 11

Detective Marcus Johnson hunched over his desk, the weak light from his lamp casting long shadows across the scattered case files. His calloused fingers traced the edges of photographs, reports, and hastily scribbled notes - fragments of a puzzle he couldn't quite piece together.

The clock ticked relentlessly in the background as Marcus muttered to himself, "There has to be a connection. John Summers, you smug bastard, I know you're behind this."

His eyes burned from hours of scrutiny, but he refused to yield. The anonymous call, the planted drugs, the ruined reputation of a dedicated teacher - it all reeked of calculated malice. And at the center of it all stood John Summers, a man whose very presence exuded an aura of untouchability.

Marcus leaned back in his chair, the creak of worn leather echoing in the empty office. "What am I missing?" he wondered, his mind racing through possibilities like a fever dream.

As if in answer, a forgotten statement caught his eye. He snatched it up, heart quickening as he read the words of a hotel employee:

"I saw Mr. Summers that day. He was... different. Nervous, like. Kept looking over his shoulder and ducking into corners. Not like himself at all."

A cold smile played across Marcus's lips. "Got you," he whispered, the thrill of the hunt coursing through his veins. But even as triumph surged within him, a nagging doubt crept in. Was this the breakthrough he sought, or merely another dead end in a labyrinth of lies?

The shadows seemed to lengthen around him, as if the very darkness conspired to conceal the truth. Marcus shook off the feeling, focusing on the task at hand. Yet he couldn't shake the sense that this case would exact a toll far beyond what he was prepared to pay.

The Oakwood Grand Hotel loomed before Detective Johnson, its gilded facade a mockery of the darkness that lurked within its walls. He strode through the revolving doors, his footsteps echoing ominously across the marble floor.

"I need to see your surveillance footage from last Tuesday," Marcus demanded, flashing his badge at the wide-eyed receptionist.

As he waited, his mind raced. What secrets would the footage reveal? And at what cost?

Minutes stretched into an eternity before the manager appeared, a nervous wreck of a man clutching a hard drive.

"Here, Detective. But I must warn you—"

Marcus snatched the drive, cutting him off. "Save your warnings. I've danced with devils before."

In the security office, Marcus hunched over a flickering screen, fast-forwarding through hours of mundane footage. His eyes burned, searching for a glimpse of—

There.

John Summers slunk into frame, his usual confidence replaced by furtive glances and trembling hands. Marcus leaned closer, pulse quickening as John disappeared into a secluded alcove.

"What are you hiding, Summers?" Marcus muttered, watching John pull out a phone.

The timestamp matched the anonymous call perfectly. Marcus's lips curled into a grim smile, but victory tasted hollow. He'd caught his prey, but at what cost to his own soul?

As he stared at John's pixelated face, Marcus couldn't shake the feeling that he'd opened a Pandora's box of secrets—ones that would haunt him long after this case was closed.

Detective Johnson's eyes narrowed as he cross-referenced the timestamp on the surveillance footage with the cell phone records sprawled before him. The numbers danced, a macabre waltz of damning evidence. John Summers' phone had pinged off a tower near

Ava's apartment the night before the anonymous call. A chill crept up Marcus's spine, the pieces of this twisted puzzle clicking into place with an almost audible snap.

"Gotcha, you smug bastard," he muttered, his voice barely a whisper in the dimly lit office.

Meanwhile, across town, Ava Jennings stood before her bathroom mirror, her reflection a stranger staring back with hollow eyes. She smoothed imaginary wrinkles from her blouse, a nervous habit that had intensified since the accusations.

"You can do this," she murmured, her voice cracking. "It's just another day."

But as she reached for the doorknob, her hand trembled. The weight of unseen eyes pressed upon her, judgment and whispers following her every move.

At the school, Ava forced a smile as she passed a group of mothers. Their conversation died abruptly, replaced by pointed silence and sidelong glances.

"Good morning," Ava said, her tone deliberately cheerful.

One mother, Sarah, nodded curtly. "Ava. Surprised to see you here."

The words hung in the air, dripping with unspoken accusations. Ava's smile faltered, but she pressed on, each step feeling like a march to the gallows.

"I'm still dedicated to our children's education," Ava replied, her voice steady despite the storm raging within. "Nothing's changed there."

Sarah's lips thinned. "Hasn't it, though?"

As Ava walked away, the whispers resumed, each one a dagger in her back. She ducked into an empty classroom, leaning against the wall as her composure crumbled.

"Why?" she whispered to the empty room. "Why is this happening to me?"

The silence offered no answers, only the echoes of her own despair.

Detective Marcus Johnson's penetrating gaze bore into John Summers across the dimly lit interrogation room. The air hung heavy with unspoken accusations, a palpable tension that seemed to pulse in the shadows.

"Mr. Summers," Johnson began, his voice a low rumble that matched the storm brewing in his eyes. "Care to explain why you were lurking near Ms. Thompson's apartment the night before the... incident?"

John's face remained an impassive mask, but a muscle twitched in his jaw. "I don't know what you're talking about, Detective," he replied, his words clipped and precise.

Johnson's lips curled into a humorless smile. He slid a folder across the table, surveillance images spilling out like dark secrets. "Let's not play games, John. We have you on camera at the Oakwood Hotel, making a very interesting phone call."

A flicker of uncertainty crossed John's face, quickly suppressed. He leaned forward, his expensive suit creasing slightly. "This is absurd. I'm a respected attorney. I demand to know what you're accusing me of."

"Respected?" Johnson chuckled, the sound devoid of mirth. "Is that what you call framing an innocent woman? Destroying her career? Her life?"

John's composure wavered, a crack in his carefully constructed facade. His mind raced, searching for an escape route that was rapidly disappearing. "You have no proof," he hissed, but the words rang hollow even to his own ears.

Johnson leaned in, his voice dropping to a whisper that seemed to echo in the oppressive silence. "Oh, but I do, John. I do."

The shrill ring of Ava's phone pierced the somber silence of her living room, echoing off walls that seemed to close in with each passing day. She stared at the screen, Detective Johnson's name glowing accusingly. With trembling fingers, she answered.

"Ms. Jennings," Johnson's gravelly voice crackled through the line, "we've had a breakthrough. I need you at the station. Now."

Ava's heart stuttered. "What kind of breakthrough?" she whispered, dread and hope warring within her.

"Not over the phone," Johnson replied, his tone brooking no argument. "Just come."

The line went dead, leaving Ava drowning in a sea of questions.

Minutes later, she found herself before the looming facade of the police station, its windows like dark, judging eyes. She hesitated, her hand on the cold metal door handle. What truths lurked beyond? What fresh horrors awaited?

Ava's mind raced, conjuring nightmarish scenarios. Had they found more evidence against her? Or perhaps... She dared not hope, yet hope bloomed treacherously in her chest.

With a deep breath that did little to calm her frayed nerves, Ava pulled open the door and stepped into the fluorescent-lit purgatory of the station's lobby. The air hung heavy with the acrid scent of cheap coffee and desperation.

Officer Ramirez glanced up from his desk, recognition flickering in his eyes. "Ms. Jennings," he nodded, "Detective Johnson's expecting you. Second door on the left."

Ava's footsteps echoed hollowly as she made her way down the corridor, each step bringing her closer to a reckoning she both craved and feared. She paused before the indicated door, her hand poised to knock. Through the frosted glass, she could make out two shadowy figures. One she recognized as Johnson's hulking form. The other...

Her breath caught in her throat. It couldn't be. Not him. Not here.

Ava's knuckles rapped against the wood before she could lose her nerve. The muffled voices within fell silent.

"Come in," Johnson's voice commanded.

With one last desperate prayer to whatever deity might be listening, Ava turned the handle and stepped into the unknown.

Detective Johnson's piercing blue eyes locked onto Ava as she entered, his grim expression a stark contrast to the triumphant gleam lurking beneath. Beside him, John Summers sat ramrod straight, his carefully cultivated mask of indifference cracking at the edges.

"Ms. Jennings," Johnson intoned, gesturing to an empty chair. "Please, have a seat."

Ava lowered herself gingerly, her gaze flickering between the two men. The air crackled with unspoken tension.

"I believe," Johnson began, his voice low and measured, "we've uncovered the truth behind your... unfortunate situation."

John's jaw clenched visibly, a muscle twitching beneath his perfectly groomed exterior.

"Mr. Summers here," Johnson continued, "has been kind enough to provide us with a full confession."

The words hung in the air, sharp and venomous. Ava's world tilted on its axis.

"I don't..." she stammered, her mind reeling. "I don't understand."

Johnson's lips curved into a humorless smile. "Allow me to illuminate. Mr. Summers orchestrated this entire charade. The anonymous call, the planted drugs – all his doing."

Ava's heart pounded, a deafening drumbeat in her ears. She turned to John, searching his face for any hint of denial, any flicker of the man she thought she knew.

"Why?" The word escaped her lips, barely a whisper.

John's eyes, once warm with false friendship, now gleamed cold and reptilian. "You were a threat," he hissed. "To my family, to our standing in the community. I couldn't allow that."

The truth crashed over Ava in waves, each revelation more devastating than the last. The carefully constructed reality she'd clung to crumbled, leaving only the stark horror of John's betrayal.

"You... you destroyed my life," Ava choked out, bile rising in her throat. "My career, my reputation – everything I've worked for..."

John's lip curled in a sneer. "Collateral damage," he spat. "You should have known your place."

Ava's world spun, darkness creeping at the edges of her vision. How deep did this malevolence run? What other shadows lurked beneath Oakwood's pristine facade?

As the full weight of John's treachery settled upon her, Ava felt something shift within her soul. The last vestiges of her naiveté withered, replaced by a cold, hard kernel of resolve. She would not be a victim. She would not let this break her.

With steel in her spine and fire in her eyes, Ava faced her tormentor. "You've made a grave mistake, John," she said, her voice steady despite the turmoil within. "And I promise you, you will regret it."

Detective Johnson's weathered hand rested on Ava's shoulder, a grounding force amidst the maelstrom of her thoughts. His voice cut through the oppressive silence, low and resolute.

"Ms. Jennings, I give you my word," he intoned, each syllable heavy with the weight of his years on the force. "John and Evelyn Summers will answer for their crimes."

Ava's gaze locked onto the detective's steely blue eyes, searching for any hint of doubt. She found none.

"How can you be so sure?" she whispered, her words barely audible in the stifling interrogation room.

Johnson's lips twisted into a grim smile. "Because people like them always leave a trail. And I've been following it for longer than they realize."

A shiver ran down Ava's spine. How long had this web of deceit been woven around her?

"We'll gather every shred of evidence," Johnson continued, his tone brooking no argument. "Every phone record, every surveillance tape, every witness statement. They thought they were clever, but their arrogance will be their undoing."

Ava's heart quickened, a spark of hope igniting in her chest. She leaned forward, her voice gaining strength.

"Thank you, Detective," she said, surpri€sed by the intensity of her own gratitude. "For believing in me when no one else would. For not giving up."

Johnson's stern features softened momentarily. "It's my job, Ms. Jennings. And it's a job I take very seriously."

As Ava stood to leave, a newfound resolve coursed through her veins. The battle ahead loomed dark and treacherous, but for the first time in months, she felt ready to face it.

Ava stepped out of the police station, the heavy doors creaking shut behind her like the closing of a tomb. The night air, thick with the promise of rain, clung to her skin. She paused, her eyes drawn to the flickering streetlamp that cast long, wavering shadows across the cracked pavement.

"One step at a time," she murmured to herself, her voice barely a whisper in the eerie stillness.

As she began her slow walk home, her mind raced with visions of the impending confrontation. John's stoic face loomed in her thoughts, his carefully measured words echoing in her ears.

"He'll try to twist everything," Ava mused, her fists clenching involuntarily. "Every word, every action... he'll make it all seem like a misunderstanding."

A car rumbled past, its headlights briefly illuminating the haunted expression on Ava's face. She shuddered, thinking of Evelyn's sharp tongue and vindictive nature.

"And Evelyn... God, what lengths will she go to?"

The thought sent a chill down Ava's spine. She quickened her pace, as if she could outrun the creeping dread that threatened to overwhelm her.

Yet, beneath the fear and uncertainty, a tiny flame of hope flickered. Ava clung to it desperately, nurturing its fragile light.

"But the truth is on my side," she whispered fiercely to the empty street. "And that has to count for something... doesn't it?"

The question hung in the air, unanswered, as Ava disappeared into the gathering darkness, the weight of her past and the uncertainty of her future pressing down upon her with each step.

Chapter 12

The empty fire station echoed with the clash of two voices, each syllable a thunderclap in the cavernous space. Carlos stood rigid, his calloused hands clenched at his sides as he faced Evelyn's fury. Her perfectly coiffed hair seemed to crackle with electricity, her designer blazer a poor shield against the inferno of her rage.

"You can't do this to me, Carlos," Evelyn hissed, her words dripping venom. "After everything we've been through?"

Carlos felt the weight of his decision pressing down on him, crushing his chest. The fluorescent lights flickered overhead, casting eerie shadows across Evelyn's contorted features. He drew a deep breath, steeling himself for what he must do.

"It's over, Evelyn," he said, his voice low and firm, yet tinged with a sadness that surprised even him. "This... whatever we had... it's become a cancer. It's eating away at everything I hold dear."

Evelyn's eyes narrowed, a predator sensing weakness. "Don't be ridiculous," she spat. "You're just scared. Weak."

Carlos flinched at her words, each one a dagger to his resolve. But he pressed on, the ghosts of his betrayals spurring him forward. "No, Evelyn. This has gone too far. It's destroying us both."

As he spoke, Carlos couldn't help but marvel at the irony. He, who had rushed into burning buildings without hesitation, now trembled before this woman and the wreckage of their affair. The station's emptiness seemed to mock him, a hollow reminder of the integrity he'd abandoned.

"Destroying us?" Evelyn laughed, a harsh, brittle sound that sent chills down Carlos's spine. "Oh, darling, you have no idea what destruction looks like. Not yet."

Carlos felt a creeping dread at her words, imagining the havoc Evelyn could wreak. But he stood his ground, haunted by the memory of his wife's trusting eyes, oblivious to his infidelity. "It ends now, Evelyn. For both our sakes."

The silence that followed was deafening, pregnant with unspoken threats and bitter regrets. In that moment, Carlos knew he had unleashed something far more dangerous than any fire he'd ever faced.

Evelyn's face contorted, her polished exterior cracking to reveal the desperation beneath. "You can't do this, Carlos," she hissed, her voice rising with each word. "We're not finished. I won't let you go."

Carlos felt a chill creep up his spine, Evelyn's words echoing in the cavernous station. He'd seen that look before – in the eyes of trapped victims, wild with fear. But this was different. Dangerous.

"It's over, Evelyn," he said, forcing steadiness into his voice. "We both knew it couldn't last."

She lunged forward, manicured nails digging into his arm. "You don't mean that. Think of everything we've shared, everything I can offer you."

Carlos gently but firmly removed her hand, his calloused fingers a stark contrast to her soft skin. "What you're offering is poison," he said, memories of stolen moments flooding his mind. "I won't destroy my family for this... whatever it is we had."

Evelyn's eyes flashed, a mix of fury and fear. "Family? That dull little life you cling to?" She laughed, the sound brittle and sharp. "I could ruin you with a single phone call, darling. Don't test me."

Carlos felt his resolve harden, even as dread pooled in his stomach. He'd faced down infernos with less trepidation than this woman's wrath. But he couldn't falter now.

"Then do it," he said quietly, meeting her gaze. "Because this ends today, no matter what."

Carlos turned, his footsteps echoing through the empty fire station like a funeral dirge. Each step away from Evelyn felt like wading through molasses, his legs leaden with the weight of guilt and relief warring within him.

"You'll regret this, Carlos Gomez," Evelyn's voice sliced through the air, sharp as a blade. "I'll make sure of it."

He didn't look back, couldn't bear to see the venom in her eyes. The station door creaked shut behind him, a final punctuation to their ill-fated affair.

The drive home was a blur, streetlights smearing like tears across his vision. Carlos gripped the steering wheel, knuckles white, as if it could anchor him against the tide of shame threatening to drown him.

As he pulled into the driveway, the porch light flickered on. His wife's silhouette appeared in the doorway, a question mark against the warm glow of home.

"Carlos?" her voice wavered as he approached. "What's wrong? You look... haunted."

He met her gaze, saw the concern etched in every line of her face. The words stuck in his throat, choking him with their weight.

"I..." he began, his voice cracking. "We need to talk."

Carlos' throat constricted, each word feeling like broken glass as he forced them out. "I've... I've done something terrible, mi amor." His gaze dropped to the floor, unable to bear the sight of trust in her eyes that he knew he was about to shatter.

His wife's brow furrowed, confusion clouding her features. "Carlos, what are you talking about? You're scaring me."

He swallowed hard, his Adams apple bobbing like a buoy in a stormy sea. "I've been... unfaithful," he whispered, the confession hanging in the air like a toxic fog.

The silence that followed was deafening. Carlos could hear his own heart pounding in his ears, a guilty rhythm that seemed to echo through the house.

When he finally mustered the courage to look up, he saw the transformation on his wife's face. The concern melted away, replaced by a kaleidoscope of emotions - shock, disbelief, anger, and finally, a soul-crushing hurt that made Carlos wish the ground would open up and swallow him whole.

"You... what?" her voice was barely audible, trembling with the effort of containing her emotions. Then, as if a dam had burst, her words came out in a torrent. "How could you? With who? For how long?" Each question was a dagger, twisting in Carlos' gut.

He stood there, absorbing her pain, knowing he deserved every ounce of it. "I'm so sorry," he managed, the words feeling pathetically inadequate. "It's over now, I swear. I ended it today."

His wife's laugh was bitter, bordering on hysterical. "Oh, you ended it today? Well, that makes everything alright then, doesn't it?" Her voice dripped with sarcasm, each word laced with venom.

Carlos reached out, a desperate attempt to bridge the chasm he'd created, but she recoiled as if his touch would burn her. The rejection stung, but he knew he had no right to feel hurt. Not now. Not after what he'd done.

Across town, Evelyn Summers sat in her pristine living room, a malevolent smile twisting her perfectly painted lips. Her manicured fingers hovered over her smartphone, poised to unleash chaos. She tapped the screen, each digit of Carlos' wife's number a step closer to her twisted goal.

The phone rang once, twice. Evelyn's heart raced with perverse anticipation. On the third ring, a confused voice answered.

"Hello?"

"Mrs. Gomez?" Evelyn purred, her tone dripping with false sweetness. "I thought you should know about your husband's... extracurricular activities."

A sharp intake of breath on the other end. "Who is this?"

Evelyn's smile widened, shark-like. "Let's just say I'm a concerned citizen. Your dear Carlos has been quite busy at the fire station, and I don't mean fighting fires."

She paused, savoring the stunned silence. In her mind's eye, she could see the woman's face crumpling, her world shattering. It was intoxicating.

"What are you talking about?" Mrs. Gomez's voice wavered, a mixture of anger and fear.

Evelyn leaned back, crossing her legs. "Oh, darling. I'm talking about the affair he's been having. Right under your nose. Isn't it time you knew the truth?"

Maria Gomez's world imploded, her heart shattering into a million jagged pieces. She stared at Carlos, her eyes brimming with tears, her voice barely above a whisper. "How could you?"

Carlos felt the weight of her gaze like a physical blow. He opened his mouth to speak, but no words came. The silence stretched between them, thick and suffocating.

"Was it all a lie?" Maria's voice cracked, raw with pain. "Every kiss, every 'I love you'... was it all just pretend while you were with her?"

Carlos shook his head, his throat constricting. "No, Maria, I—"

"Don't!" she spat, her pain morphing into rage. "Don't you dare try to explain this away!"

He reached for her, but she recoiled as if his touch would burn. "Please, just let me—"

"How long?" Maria demanded, her eyes flashing. "How long have you been betraying our vows?"

Carlos felt the weight of his sins crushing him. "Six months," he whispered, the confession tasting like ash in his mouth.

Maria's laugh was hollow, haunting. "Six months of lies. Of coming home to me, of sleeping in our bed, all while you were—" She broke off, unable to finish the thought.

"I'm sorry," Carlos breathed, the words woefully inadequate. "I never meant to hurt you."

"But you did," Maria said, her voice cold and distant. "You destroyed everything we built."

Carlos stood there, a broken man, as the love of his life turned away, leaving him alone with the ghost of what they once were.

The silence that fell between them was deafening, punctuated only by Maria's stifled sobs and Carlos's ragged breathing. Shadows crept across the room, darkening the corners and seeming to close in on them both.

Carlos's mind raced, desperately searching for words to mend the chasm he'd created. "Maria, I—" he began, but his voice faltered, the weight of his betrayal choking him.

Maria turned to face him, her eyes glassy with unshed tears. "Don't," she whispered, her voice barely audible. "Just... don't."

The air grew thick with unspoken accusations and shattered trust. Carlos felt the walls of their home—once a sanctuary—now closing in, suffocating him with memories of happier times.

"What now?" Maria asked, her gaze fixed on a point beyond Carlos, as if she couldn't bear to look at him directly.

Carlos swallowed hard, his hands trembling at his sides. "I don't know," he admitted, the words tasting bitter on his tongue.

As night fell outside, casting long shadows across their living room, the reality of their situation settled over them like a shroud. Their voices faded to nothing, leaving only the hollow echo of what they once were—and the haunting whisper of what they had become.

Chapter 13

The shadows stretched long across Ava Jennings' office as twilight crept in through the blinds. She sat motionless behind her desk, staring out at the empty playground of Pine View Elementary. The cheerful laughter of children felt like a distant memory now.

Ava's fingers traced absent patterns on the smooth oak surface before her. Her eyes, once bright with enthusiasm, now held a weary darkness. The past year's events played through her mind like a grainy film reel, each frame etched with pain.

"How did it come to this?" she whispered to the empty room.

The silence offered no reply, only the faint echo of her own voice. Ava's shoulders sagged under an invisible weight. The relentless campaign waged against her had taken its toll, chipping away at her spirit day by day.

She closed her eyes, willing herself to find strength. "I can't let them win. The children need me."

But even as the words left her lips, doubt crept in like a chill. How much more could she endure? The vindictive couple's attacks seemed endless, each one more vicious than the last.

Ava's gaze drifted to the family photos lining her desk. Smiling faces stared back at her, frozen in happier times. A lump formed in her throat.

"I'm sorry," she murmured, touching a frame gently. "I never meant for any of this to touch you."

The ticking of the wall clock punctuated the heavy silence. Tick. Tock. Tick. Tock. Each second that passed felt like another nail in the coffin of her once-pristine reputation.

Ava's jaw clenched, a flicker of determination sparking in her eyes. She straightened her posture, squaring her shoulders against the weight of her burdens.

"No," she said firmly, her voice stronger now. "I won't let them break me. This school, these children - they're worth fighting for."

But even as resolve steeled her spine, a treacherous voice whispered from the recesses of her mind: *How long can you keep fighting a losing battle?*

The harsh fluorescent lights of the police station seared Ava's retinas as she blinked back tears. Her wrists chafed against the cold metal of the handcuffs, a physical reminder of her sudden fall from grace.

"I swear, Officer, those aren't mine," Ava pleaded, her voice cracking. "I've never seen those drugs before in my life."

The detective's face remained impassive. "Ma'am, we found them in your vehicle. Can you explain that?"

Ava's mind raced, desperately grasping for an explanation that wouldn't come. Her stomach churned as realization dawned - this was no accident, no misunderstanding. This was sabotage.

"I... I can't," she whispered, defeat washing over her like a tidal wave.

As they led her away, Ava caught sight of her reflection in a window. The woman staring back at her was a stranger - pale, disheveled, eyes wild with disbelief.

Back in her dimly lit office, Ava's fingers trembled as she traced the outline of her face in an old photograph. "Was there something I missed?" she murmured. "A sign I should have seen?"

The silence offered no answers, only amplifying the doubts that echoed in her mind. Had her trusting nature been her downfall? Should she have been more vigilant, more suspicious?

"Maybe if I'd been more careful," Ava whispered, her voice barely audible. "If I'd locked my car, or... or..."

But even as she spoke, a part of her knew it was futile. The couple's vendetta ran too deep, their methods too insidious. They would have found another way, another weakness to exploit.

Ava's gaze drifted to the window, where shadows danced across the schoolyard. "How did it come to this?" she wondered aloud, her words hanging heavy in the air.

The shrill ring of the school bell pierced the somber silence, jolting Ava from her reverie. She blinked, realizing she'd been lost in the labyrinth of her thoughts again. With a deep breath, she smoothed her blouse and stepped into the bustling hallway.

A sea of small faces greeted her, their eyes bright with innocence untouched by the shadows that haunted her. Little Emma, her pigtails bouncing, rushed up to Ava, brandishing a crayon drawing.

"Mrs. Jennings! Look what I made for you!"

Ava's lips curved into a genuine smile, the first in what felt like an eternity. "It's beautiful, Emma. Thank you."

As she pinned the colorful creation to her office wall, a warmth bloomed in her chest, pushing back the chill of despair. The children's laughter echoed through the corridors, a balm to her wounded spirit.

Later, in the teacher's lounge, Mrs. Thompson approached, her kind eyes crinkling with concern. "Ava, dear, how are you holding up?"

Ava's facade wavered. "I'm... managing," she whispered, her voice threatening to crack.

Mrs. Thompson placed a comforting hand on her shoulder. "Remember, darkness can't drive out darkness. Only light can do that."

Ava nodded, drawing strength from the older woman's unwavering support. "Sometimes," she confessed, "I feel like I'm drowning in shadows."

"Then we'll be your lighthouse," Mrs. Thompson replied, her voice steady and sure. "Every storm passes, Ava. And you're stronger than you know."

As they spoke, Ava felt a flicker of hope ignite within her. Perhaps, with allies like Mrs. Thompson and the children's unbridled joy, she could weather this tempest after all.

The clock's relentless ticking echoed through Ava's dimly lit bedroom, each second a mocking reminder of her torment. She curled into herself, shoulders shaking with silent sobs. The weight of the vindictive couple's actions pressed down on her chest, threatening to suffocate her very essence.

"I can't... I can't do this anymore," she whispered to the empty room, her voice cracking like brittle glass.

Memories flooded her mind, unbidden and merciless. The shocked faces of her colleagues as the police led her away. The whispers that followed her through the grocery store aisles. The pitying glances from parents who once admired her.

Ava's fingers clutched at her bedsheets, knuckles white with desperation. "What's the point?" she murmured, darkness seeping into her thoughts. "They've won. They've taken everything."

But as the shadows threatened to consume her, a small voice in the back of her mind whispered, "Not everything. Not yet."

Ava's breath caught. She sat up slowly, wiping tears from her cheeks with trembling hands. "No," she said, her voice barely audible. "Not yet."

She stood, legs unsteady, and made her way to the mirror. The woman staring back at her was a stranger – hollow-eyed and haunted. But there, in the depths of her gaze, a spark of defiance flickered to life.

"Enough," Ava declared, her voice growing stronger. "I won't let them destroy me. I won't let them win."

She straightened her shoulders, chin lifting with newfound resolve. "The truth will come out," she vowed to her reflection. "And when it does, they'll be the ones running scared."

As dawn's first light crept through the curtains, Ava felt a shift within herself. The darkness still lingered, but now it fueled her determination. She would fight back, not just for herself, but for every child at Pine View who deserved better than to be caught in this web of deceit.

"Game on," Ava whispered, a grim smile tugging at her lips. The vindictive couple had no idea what they'd awakened in her. And she intended to show them, one carefully calculated step at a time.

Ava smoothed her blouse, hands trembling slightly as she approached the community center. The autumn fair buzzed with activity, a stark contrast to the desolation that had consumed her for months. She hesitated at the entrance, heart racing.

"You can do this," she whispered to herself, forcing a smile that didn't quite reach her eyes.

As she stepped inside, Mrs. Thompson's familiar voice rang out. "Ava! So glad you could make it."

Ava's smile became a fraction more genuine. "Wouldn't miss it for the world," she replied, her voice steady despite the churning in her stomach.

She moved through the crowd, engaging in small talk with parents and colleagues. Each interaction felt like walking on eggshells, but Ava persevered.

"How are the kids enjoying the new library books, Mr. Jacobs?" she asked, carefully maintaining eye contact.

"Oh, they're loving them!" he enthused. "Your fundraising efforts really paid off."

A warmth bloomed in Ava's chest, momentarily eclipsing the darkness. She'd made a difference, despite everything.

As the fair progressed, Ava found herself relaxing incrementally. The familiar routines of community engagement anchored her, providing a lifeline to the person she used to be.

But beneath the surface, doubts gnawed at her. Every smile felt like a mask, every laugh a performance. The weight of her ordeal pressed down, threatening to crack her carefully constructed facade.

"You okay?" Mrs. Thompson asked quietly, catching Ava's arm as she passed.

Ava's mask slipped for a moment, revealing the turmoil beneath. Then, with practiced ease, she rebuilt her walls. "Never better," she lied smoothly, her smile not quite reaching her eyes. "Now, shall we announce the raffle winners?"

Ava stood by the window, her reflection a ghostly apparition in the twilight. The school fair's excitement had faded, leaving her alone with her thoughts. She traced a finger along the windowsill, feeling the grooves worn by time.

"I'm not who I was," she whispered to the empty room, her voice barely audible. "But maybe... that's not entirely bad."

The memory of the vindictive couple's actions still stung, a wound not fully healed. Yet, as she gazed at her reflection, Ava saw something new in her eyes - a steely determination that hadn't been there before.

She turned from the window, her gaze falling on the stack of thank-you notes from students. A bitter smile tugged at her lips.

"Who would've thought," she mused, "that their cruelty would forge me into... this?"

The phone on her desk buzzed. Mrs. Thompson's name flashed on the screen.

"Ava?" came the concerned voice. "How are you holding up?"

Ava paused, weighing her words. "I'm... different, Sarah. Scarred, but stronger."

"That's my girl," Mrs. Thompson replied, her tone warm. "You've come so far."

"Have I?" Ava's laugh was hollow. "Sometimes I feel like I'm still that woman, watching her world crumble as they planted those drugs in my car."

"But you're not, Ava. You're so much more now."

Ava's gaze drifted back to the window, to the darkening sky beyond. "You're right," she said softly. "I am."

As she hung up, a strange calm settled over her. She took a deep breath, feeling the tension in her shoulders ease.

"Time to end this," she murmured, her eyes gleaming with newfound resolve. "Once and for all."

The shadows lengthened across Ava's office as twilight crept in, casting an eerie pall over the room. She reached for her bag, her movements deliberate, almost predatory.

"Tomorrow," she whispered, her voice a ghostly echo in the empty space. "Tomorrow, we dance."

As she locked her office door, a chill wind whipped through the hallway, carrying whispers of impending confrontation. Ava paused, her hand still on the doorknob, a shiver crawling up her spine.

"Mrs. Jennings?" A small voice startled her.

She turned to find Tommy, a third-grader, his eyes wide with concern. "Are you okay? You look... different."

Ava's lips curved into a smile that didn't quite reach her eyes. "I'm fine, Tommy. Just... preparing for a big day."

"Is it about the mean people?" he asked innocently.

Her breath caught. "What do you know about that?"

Tommy shrugged. "My mom says they're trying to hurt you. But you're too nice to hurt, Mrs. Jennings."

Ava knelt down, her heart heavy. "Sometimes, Tommy, even nice people have to fight back."

As the child nodded and scampered away, Ava straightened, her resolve hardening. The innocence of children, she thought, was a luxury she could no longer afford.

She stepped into the gathering dusk, the night air thick with foreboding. Tomorrow loomed, a dark promise on the horizon. The final act was about to begin.

Chapter 14

A pale beam of moonlight crept across Ava's face, rousing her from fitful dreams. Her eyes snapped open, heart pounding with renewed resolve. The revelations of yesterday swirled in her mind like wisps of fog, slowly coalescing into clarity.

She reached for her phone with trembling fingers, its glow harsh in the pre-dawn gloom. Ava typed swiftly, urgency driving away the last vestiges of sleep:

"We need to meet. Our next move is critical. The usual place, 8 AM."

The message to Detective Johnson sent with a soft chime. Ava stared at the screen, willing a response. Seconds stretched into minutes, each tick of the clock an eternity.

Finally, a reply: "I'll be there."

Relief washed over her, tinged with a hint of foreboding. What dark truths would this day reveal?

Hours later, Ava pushed open the door of The Broken Mug, a dingy coffee shop on the outskirts of town. The bell's jingle seemed to mock the gravity of her purpose. Stale coffee and secrets permeated the air.

Detective Johnson sat hunched in a shadowy corner, his piercing gaze fixed on her approach. Ava slid into the booth, its cracked vinyl a stark reminder of better days long past.

"You look like hell, Ava," Johnson growled, his voice low and gravelly.

She managed a wan smile. "Charming as ever, Detective. Sleep isn't a luxury I can afford these days."

Johnson's eyes narrowed. "None of us can. Not with what's at stake."

Ava leaned in, her voice barely above a whisper. "So, what's our next move? How do we bring them down?"

The detective's pause stretched uncomfortably. Ava's stomach churned with dread. What wasn't he telling her?

"We need hard evidence," Johnson finally said. "Something concrete to link Evelyn and John to the conspiracy."

Ava's mind raced. How far was she willing to go? The weight of her choices pressed down upon her, a suffocating blanket of responsibility.

"Whatever it takes," she heard herself say, the words tasting of ash and regret. "I won't let them destroy everything I've built."

Johnson nodded grimly. "Then we have work to do."

As they bent their heads together, plotting in hushed tones, Ava couldn't shake the feeling that she was selling pieces of her soul with every whispered plan. But there was no turning back now. The die was cast, and darkness lay ahead.

Johnson pulled a folded document from his jacket, sliding it across the table with a furtive glance. "I've secured a search warrant for the Summers' residence," he murmured, his voice barely audible above the coffee shop's ambient hum.

Ava's heart raced as she scanned the official letterhead. "How did you manage this?" she whispered, her fingers trembling slightly as they traced the edges of the paper.

"Let's just say I called in a few favors," Johnson replied, his eyes betraying a flicker of something darker. "We need to find anything that ties them to this mess. Letters, emails, financial records – anything that proves their involvement."

Ava nodded, her throat tight with anticipation and fear. "When do we move?"

Johnson leaned back, his face half-hidden in shadow. "That's where it gets tricky. We can't risk them being home. We need to catch them off guard, vulnerable."

"A social event, perhaps?" Ava suggested, her mind racing through possibilities. "Or when they're out of town?"

"Exactly," Johnson agreed, a grim smile playing at the corners of his mouth. "We wait for the perfect moment, then strike."

As they continued to plot in hushed tones, Ava couldn't shake the feeling that she was crossing a line she could never uncross. The weight of their conspiracy pressed down on her, a suffocating blanket of guilt and necessity. But what choice did she have? The Summers had started this war, and she would finish it – no matter the cost to her soul.

The pale moon hung like a watchful eye as Ava crouched in the shadows of a gnarled oak, her breath misting in the chill night air. Detective Johnson's hulking form loomed beside her, his weathered face etched with lines of concentration. For days, they had stalked their prey, two vengeful spirits haunting the periphery of Evelyn and John's lives.

"They're creatures of habit," Johnson murmured, his voice a low rumble. "Every Tuesday, 8 PM sharp, they leave for their country club soirée. Like clockwork."

Ava's heart quickened, a war drum in her chest. "And we're certain they won't return early?"

Johnson's eyes glinted in the darkness. "As certain as we can be in this godforsaken game."

The Summers' mansion loomed before them, a grotesque monument to wealth and secrets. Ava's fingers curled around the cold metal of the lockpicking tools, instruments of her own damnation.

"Ready?" Johnson asked, his hand hovering over her shoulder, not quite touching.

Ava swallowed hard, tasting bile. "As I'll ever be."

They glided across the manicured lawn, shadows among shadows. At the back door, Ava's trembling hands worked the lock, each click an accusation. *What have I become?* she wondered, as the tumblers yielded to her touch.

The door swung open with a mournful creak. Ava hesitated on the threshold, her conscience screaming in protest.

"Second thoughts?" Johnson's voice was tinged with something unreadable – concern? Disappointment?

Ava steeled herself, stepping into the dark maw of the house. "No," she lied, the word bitter on her tongue. "Let's finish this."

As they slipped inside, Ava couldn't shake the feeling that she was leaving a piece of her soul behind on that doorstep, a sacrifice to the altar of vengeance.

The cavernous interior of the Summers' home swallowed them whole, shadows clinging to their forms like a second skin. Ava's eyes darted nervously, half-expecting Evelyn's polished figure to materialize from the gloom.

"We'll cover more ground separately," Johnson whispered, his voice barely a breath. "You take the study, I'll search the master bedroom."

Ava nodded, her throat too dry for words. As Johnson's footsteps faded upstairs, she crept towards John's study, each step an act of betrayal against her former self.

The study door yielded easily, and Ava slipped inside. Moonlight filtered through heavy curtains, casting long fingers across the room. She began her methodical search, rifling through drawers and cabinets with trembling hands.

What am I looking for? she wondered, desperation clawing at her chest. *What could possibly justify this invasion?*

As if in answer, her fingers brushed against something out of place – a slight indentation in the back of a drawer. Heart pounding, Ava pried at the false bottom until it gave way with a soft click.

There, nestled in the hidden compartment, lay a stack of letters and photographs. Ava's breath caught as she recognized her own face staring back at her from glossy prints, surveillance photos taken without her knowledge.

"Oh God," she whispered, horror and vindication warring within her. With shaking hands, she began snapping pictures of the evidence with her phone, each click of the camera sealing Evelyn and John's fate.

As she worked, a quiet voice in the back of her mind whispered: *And what of your fate, Ava? What demons have you unleashed in pursuit of justice?*

Detective Johnson's practiced fingers danced over the safe's dial, his ear pressed close to its cold metal surface. Each faint click sent a shiver down his spine, a grim reminder of the secrets that lay hidden within.

"Come on, you bastard," he muttered, his voice barely audible in the oppressive silence of John's study.

With a final, decisive turn, the safe surrendered its contents. Johnson's eyes widened as he beheld a trove of financial records and bank statements, each page a damning piece of evidence against Evelyn and John.

How deep does this rabbit hole go? he wondered, a chill settling in his bones.

Meanwhile, Ava's footsteps echoed softly as she made her way back to Johnson. Her heart raced, the weight of her discoveries pressing down upon her like a shroud.

"Detective," she whispered, her voice quavering. "I found something."

Johnson turned, his face a mask of grim satisfaction. "So did I, Ms. Jennings. It seems our friends have been quite busy."

They huddled together, carefully examining their findings. Ava's hands trembled as she held up her phone, displaying the incriminating photos.

"My God," Johnson breathed. "This is bigger than we thought."

Ava nodded, her voice barely above a whisper. "What have we stumbled into, Detective?"

As they gathered the evidence, taking care to leave no trace of their presence, a sense of foreboding settled over them. The truth they sought now seemed a double-edged sword, promising justice but threatening to cut them deeply in the process.

The shadows lengthened, stretching across the room like grasping fingers as Ava and Detective Johnson conducted their final sweep. Every creak of the floorboards sent a jolt through Ava's nerves, her imagination conjuring spectral guardians of the Summers' secrets.

"We can't afford to miss anything," Johnson murmured, his keen eyes scanning the room. "The devil's in the details."

Ava nodded, her throat tight. "It feels like the walls are watching us," she whispered.

Johnson's lips twitched in a humorless smile. "Walls have ears, Ms. Jennings. But we've been quieter than ghosts."

With practiced efficiency, they erased all traces of their intrusion. As they slipped out the back door, Ava's hand trembled on the lock. The soft click as it engaged sounded like a gunshot in the eerie silence.

"It's done," she breathed, relief and dread warring within her.

The drive to their meeting place was tense, the weight of their ill-gotten evidence heavy between them. In a dimly lit corner of a nondescript diner, they spread out their findings like a macabre feast.

"These financial records," Johnson muttered, his brow furrowed. "They're laundering money through shell companies. But why?"

Ava's eyes widened as she connected the dots. "The PTA funds... they've been siphoning them off for years."

Johnson's gaze met hers, a spark of understanding igniting. "And using your position as a scapegoat. Clever bastards."

"How do we prove it?" Ava asked, her voice barely above a whisper. "They'll bury us if we don't get this right."

Johnson's face was grim. "We build an airtight case. Every 'i' dotted, every 't' crossed. Then we take it straight to the DA."

As they pored over the evidence, Ava couldn't shake the feeling that they'd opened Pandora's box. The truth was within their grasp, but at what cost?

The diner's fluorescent lights flickered ominously, casting ghastly shadows across their faces. Ava's fingers trembled as she traced the outline of a particularly damning photograph.

"We need to meet again," Detective Johnson said, his voice low and gravelly. "Thursday. Same time, same place. We'll finalize our strategy then."

Ava nodded, her throat tight. "And if they suspect something before then?"

Johnson's eyes gleamed with a mix of determination and something darker. "Then we accelerate our timeline. Remember, Ava, we're not the villains here."

A bitter laugh escaped her lips. "Aren't we? Breaking and entering, theft..."

"Sometimes," he murmured, "the path to justice isn't straight."

As they parted ways, Ava felt a chill settle deep in her bones. The parking lot seemed to stretch endlessly before her, each shadow a potential threat.

In her car, she gripped the steering wheel until her knuckles turned white. The evidence they'd gathered felt like a ticking time bomb in her bag. As she navigated the empty streets, her mind raced.

"What if we're wrong?" she whispered to herself. "What if this destroys everything?"

Images of Evelyn's polished smile and John's calculating gaze flashed through her mind. The depth of their betrayal made her stomach churn.

Yet, beneath the anxiety, a flicker of excitement burned. They were close - so close - to exposing the truth. To reclaiming her life and her reputation.

As she approached her neighborhood, a car in her rearview mirror caught her attention. Was it following her, or was her paranoia getting the best of her?

Ava's heart raced as she turned onto her street, the shadows of the trees looming like specters in the night.

The key trembled in Ava's hand as she approached her front door. The porch light flickered ominously, casting grotesque shadows across the once-welcoming facade. She paused, her breath catching in her throat as a floorboard creaked behind her.

"Just the wind," she muttered, but her voice sounded hollow even to her own ears.

Inside, the house felt different - colder, somehow. Ava's fingers fumbled for the light switch, her eyes darting to every corner.

"Pull yourself together," she chided, but her heart continued its frantic rhythm.

As she moved through the living room, a framed photo caught her eye. It was from last year's school fundraiser - Evelyn's arm draped casually over her shoulder, both women beaming at the camera. Ava's stomach lurched.

"How long were you plotting against me?" she whispered, her voice barely audible.

The silence that answered seemed to mock her.

Ava sank onto the couch, her body suddenly heavy with exhaustion. She closed her eyes, trying to steady her breathing.

"I can do this," she murmured. "I'm not alone. Detective Johnson believes in me. We have evidence."

But as she opened her eyes, the shadows in the room seemed to deepen, reaching out with spectral fingers.

"What if it's not enough?" The thought slithered through her mind, insidious and persistent.

Ava shook her head, forcing herself to stand. "No. We'll bring them to justice. We have to."

She moved to the window, peering out at the quiet street. The night seemed to press against the glass, full of secrets and threats.

"Whatever comes next," Ava whispered, her breath fogging the pane, "I'm ready."

But even as she spoke the words, a chill ran down her spine. The battle ahead loomed, dark and uncertain, and Ava couldn't shake the feeling that this was only the beginning of her nightmare.

Chapter 15

The wail of sirens shattered the oppressive silence of Oakwood's most prestigious neighborhood. Flashing red and blue lights bathed Evelyn and John Summers' palatial home in an eerie glow, transforming the manicured lawn into a sinister stage.

Evelyn's perfectly coiffed hair fell in disarray as she stumbled onto the front steps, her designer silk robe billowing in the night breeze. John emerged behind her, his usual commanding presence diminished, shoulders slumped beneath his tailored pajamas.

"This is preposterous," Evelyn hissed, her voice dripping with venom. "Do you have any idea who we are?"

The lead officer approached, his face an impassive mask. "Mr. and Mrs. Summers, you're under arrest."

John's mind raced, searching for an escape. We've covered our tracks. There's no evidence. This can't be happening.

As cold metal handcuffs clicked shut around her wrists, Evelyn's carefully constructed facade crumbled. "You can't do this to us! We were protecting our son!"

Neighbors peered from behind curtains, hungry for a glimpse of the spectacle unfolding. Evelyn locked eyes with Mrs. Patterson across the street, seeing a mixture of shock and schadenfreude in the woman's gaze.

They're enjoying this, Evelyn realized with mounting horror. All these years of cowering before us, and now they revel in our downfall.

John remained silent as they were led to separate police cars, his legal mind already formulating strategies. We'll weather this storm. We always do.

But as the cars pulled away, sirens fading into the distance, a chill settled over Oakwood. The mighty had fallen, and the whispers began.

In the local diner, forks clattered against plates as patrons devoured the news with their morning coffee.

"Can you believe it?" Mrs. Johnson exclaimed, her eyes wide. "The Summers, arrested! What will happen to poor Oliver now?"

Mr. Peterson, a retired teacher, snorted derisively. "Poor Oliver? That boy's been just as much a terror as his parents. The apple doesn't fall far from the tree."

Across town, in the teacher's lounge of Oakwood Elementary, a weight lifted from shoulders long bowed by the Summers' reign of terror.

"I never thought I'd see the day," Ms. Thompson murmured, her hands shaking slightly as she poured her coffee.

Mr. Harris, the principal, nodded solemnly. "It's been a long time coming. Maybe now we can focus on education instead of lawsuit prevention."

As dawn broke over Oakwood, a tentative hope bloomed. The town's tormentors had fallen, but the scars of their reign would linger, a constant reminder of how easily power could corrupt and how swiftly justice could strike.

Detective Marcus Johnson stood before the gathered crowd, his weathered face a mask of grim determination. The room, thick with tension, fell silent as he began to speak.

"Ladies and gentlemen," he intoned, his voice low and gravelly, "what I'm about to show you will shake the very foundations of Oakwood."

With a click, the projector hummed to life, casting an eerie glow across the faces of the stunned onlookers. Images flickered across the screen - surveillance photos, bank statements, intercepted emails. Each piece of evidence another nail in the Summers' coffin.

"My God," someone whispered, the words barely audible over the collective gasp that rippled through the room.

Johnson's eyes narrowed as he continued, "Phone records show numerous calls to known criminals. Financial documents reveal a complex web of bribes and blackmail."

As he spoke, John Summers' carefully constructed world crumbled around him. Sitting in the stark interrogation room, he felt the weight of his sins pressing down upon him. His mind raced, searching for an escape route that no longer existed.

"This can't be happening," he thought, his usually impeccable appearance now disheveled. "We were untouchable."

Beside him, Evelyn's composure had shattered completely. Her polished exterior gave way to raw, unbridled fury.

"You bastards!" she shrieked, lunging at the two-way mirror. "This is all lies! You can't do this to us!"

John reached out, grasping her arm. "Evelyn, please," he pleaded, his voice cracking. "Don't make this worse."

But as he looked into her wild eyes, John knew it was already too late. Their reign of terror had come to an inglorious end, leaving behind a legacy of fear and broken lives.

Ava's heart pounded in her chest as she watched Evelyn and John being led away in handcuffs, their once-imposing figures now diminished and pathetic. A chill ran down her spine, equal parts relief and lingering dread.

"It's over," she whispered, her voice barely audible.

Detective Johnson approached, his face etched with grim satisfaction. "You did well, Ava. Your testimony was crucial."

She nodded, unable to tear her eyes away from the retreating forms of her tormentors. "Will it be enough?"

"More than enough," Johnson replied, his tone resolute. "They won't hurt anyone else."

Ava's mind reeled, memories of sleepless nights and constant paranoia flooding back. "I never thought... never dreamed we'd actually..."

"Justice has a way of catching up," Johnson mused, his weathered face softening slightly. "Even to those who think they're above it."

As they spoke, a crowd began to gather. Whispers and murmurs rippled through the onlookers, a palpable shift in the air.

"Is it true?" Mrs. Henderson, the local librarian, asked hesitantly. "Were they really behind everything?"

Ava nodded, her throat tight. "Yes. All of it."

The crowd's reaction was a symphony of gasps, relieved sighs, and muttered curses. Ava felt the weight of their stares, a mix of sympathy and newfound respect.

"What happens now?" someone called out.

Ava gazed at the familiar faces of her neighbors, seeing hope where there had once been fear. "We heal," she said softly. "We rebuild."

As the words left her lips, Ava felt a flicker of something she hadn't dared feel in months: hope.

The courthouse loomed before Ava, its stone façade a silent witness to the day's proceedings. She inhaled sharply, steeling herself for what lay ahead.

Inside, the courtroom buzzed with nervous energy. Ava's eyes darted to Evelyn and John, their once-impeccable appearance now disheveled. Evelyn's mascara ran in dark rivulets, while John's jaw clenched rhythmically.

"All rise," the bailiff's voice cut through the murmurs.

As the judge entered, Ava's heart pounded. She thought, "This is it. The moment we've fought for."

The verdict came swiftly, each word a hammer blow. "Guilty on all counts."

Applause erupted, a cathartic release of pent-up emotion. Ava remained still, watching as Evelyn crumbled.

"This isn't over!" Evelyn shrieked, her polished veneer shattered. "You'll all pay!"

John, ever the stoic, simply closed his eyes in resignation.

Detective Johnson leaned in, whispering, "You did it, Ava. It's over."

But was it? Ava wondered, a chill running down her spine. The damage done, the trust shattered – could it truly be mended?

Outside, bathed in weak sunlight, Ava faced her future. The weight of the past year lifted, yet left an indelible mark.

"What now?" she mused aloud, her voice barely audible.

A gentle hand on her shoulder startled her. Mrs. Henderson smiled warmly. "We move forward, dear. Together."

Ava nodded, a tentative smile forming. The road ahead was long, but no longer shrouded in darkness.

The autumn breeze whispered through Oakwood's streets, carrying with it the scent of change. Ava stood at the edge of the town square, watching as volunteers hung colorful banners for the upcoming Fall Festival. A bittersweet smile played on her lips.

"It's strange, isn't it?" Principal Davis's voice startled her from her reverie. "Seeing life go on?"

Ava nodded, her eyes fixed on the bustling scene. "I keep waiting for the other shoe to drop," she confessed, her voice barely above a whisper.

Davis sighed. "We all do, in a way. But that's why this," he gestured to the preparations, "is so important."

A child's laughter rang out, piercing through Ava's melancholy. She recognized Oliver Summers, playing with other children near the gazebo. The sight twisted her heart.

"How is he coping?" she asked, unable to look away.

"As well as can be expected," Davis replied. "Children are resilient, but..."

"But the scars remain," Ava finished, her voice hollow.

She watched as Oliver stumbled, scraping his knee. Before she could move, Mrs. Henderson was there, comforting the boy with gentle words and a bandage produced from her ever-present purse.

"We're all looking out for each other now," Davis mused. "It's a start."

Ava's mind drifted to the dark days of isolation and suspicion. "A start," she echoed, "but the shadows linger."

As if on cue, a cool gust extinguished the warm glow of a nearby lantern, plunging a corner of the square into darkness. Ava shivered, wondering if Oakwood would ever truly shake off the chill of Evelyn and John's reign of terror.

Chapter 16

The courtroom loomed like a mausoleum, its hushed whispers a funeral dirge. Ava's heart fluttered in her chest, a caged bird yearning for freedom. She stole furtive glances at Evelyn and John, their faces masks of stone.

"It's almost over," Ava reminded herself, her nails digging crescents into her palms. But was it? Or would their influence reach beyond these walls, haunting her still?

Evelyn's perfectly coiffed hair gleamed under the harsh fluorescents. John's jaw clenched rhythmically, the only sign of turmoil beneath his impeccable suit.

"All rise," the bailiff's voice cracked like a whip.

They stood as one, a sea of suits and expectations. The judge entered, robes billowing like the wings of some great carrion bird. Silence fell, oppressive and absolute.

"Your Honor," John murmured, inclining his head with practiced deference.

Ava's breath caught. Would he find a way to twist the truth even now? To slither free of justice's grasp?

The judge's gavel fell with the finality of a coffin lid closing. "Be seated."

As they sank into their chairs, Ava felt the weight of inevitability settle over her. Whatever came next would shape the course of all their lives. She closed her eyes, remembering the long nights, the whispered threats, the constant fear...

"We gather today," the judge intoned, "to determine the fate of Evelyn and John Summers."

Ava's eyes snapped open. This was it. The moment of reckoning had arrived at last.

The judge's voice cut through the suffocating silence like a razor. "Evelyn and John Summers, you stand accused of harassment, defamation, and conspiracy to harm Ava Jennings. The evidence against you is substantial."

Ava's heart thundered in her chest, each beat a reminder of the countless sleepless nights she'd endured. She watched as Evelyn's perfectly manicured nails dug into the polished wood of the defendant's table.

"Before I pass judgment," the judge continued, "you have one final opportunity to address this court. Mrs. Summers?"

Evelyn rose, her designer suit a armor of wealth and privilege. Her eyes, cold as winter frost, swept across the courtroom before settling on Ava. "I did what any mother would do," she hissed, venom dripping from every syllable. "I protected my child."

Ava suppressed a shudder, remembering the relentless campaign of terror Evelyn had waged.

"And you, Mr. Summers?" the judge prompted.

John stood, his composure cracking ever so slightly. A bead of sweat trickled down his temple. "Your Honor, I-" he began, his usual eloquence faltering.

Evelyn cut him off. "We plead guilty," she spat, her voice trembling with barely contained rage.

The courtroom erupted in hushed whispers. Ava's world tilted on its axis. After all this time, after all the pain and fear, to hear those words...

"Evelyn," John hissed, but it was too late.

Ava's vision blurred, relief and disbelief warring within her. She'd imagined this moment a thousand times, but the reality was so much more... hollow.

As Evelyn's bitter admission echoed in her ears, Ava realized that justice, long-awaited, tasted more like ashes than sweet victory.

The judge's gavel cracked through the air, silencing the murmurs. "Very well," he intoned, his voice heavy with the weight of judgment. "Mrs. Summers, given the severity of your actions and the lasting harm inflicted upon Ms. Jennings and her family, I sentence you to eight years in state prison."

Ava's breath caught in her throat. Relief flooded her veins, chased by an unexpected pang of... was it pity? She watched Evelyn's perfectly manicured hands clench into fists, knuckles white against the rich mahogany of the table.

"Furthermore," the judge continued, "you are to have no contact with Ms. Jennings or her family upon your release."

A strangled sound escaped Evelyn's lips, part laugh, part sob. Ava felt a chill creep down her spine. Even now, facing the consequences of her actions, Evelyn's eyes burned with a fierce, unrepentant fire.

John stood then, his usual commanding presence diminished. "Your Honor," he began, his voice cracking slightly, "I... I also plead guilty."

Ava leaned forward, heart pounding. She'd waited so long to see the mighty John Summers brought low.

"I allowed my position and influence to..." John faltered, swallowing hard. "To perpetrate a grave injustice."

For a moment, the mask slipped. Ava saw not the ruthless attorney, but a man realizing the full weight of his choices. It was almost... pitiful.

"Mr. Summers," the judge said, "your position as an officer of the court makes your actions particularly egregious. Do you understand the consequences you now face?"

John nodded, a slight tremor in his usually steady hands. "I do, Your Honor."

Ava watched, a tangle of emotions knotting in her chest. Justice, yes, but at what cost? The ruins of lives lay scattered before her, and she wondered if anyone truly emerged victorious from such devastation.

The judge's gavel cracked like thunder, echoing through the courtroom. "John Summers, for your role in this conspiracy and abuse of power, I sentence you to eight years in federal prison."

Ava's breath caught in her throat. A surge of vindication coursed through her veins, dark and heady. She watched John's shoulders slump, his carefully constructed facade crumbling like ancient ruins.

"Additionally," the judge continued, her voice as cold and unyielding as winter frost, "you are hereby disbarred and prohibited from practicing law in any capacity for life."

A soft gasp escaped Ava's lips. John Summers, the man who'd wielded his legal prowess like a weapon, now stood stripped of his power. His empire of influence, built on lies and manipulation, lay in ashes at his feet.

As the full weight of the sentence settled over the courtroom, Ava's gaze darted between John and Evelyn. Their eyes met, a fleeting moment charged with unspoken accusations and bitter realizations.

Evelyn's lip curled in disgust, her voice a venomous whisper. "This is your fault."

John's response was equally caustic. "We're both to blame, darling. How does it feel to be on the losing side for once?"

Ava watched their exchange, a chill creeping through her bones. The Summers' marriage, once a fortress of wealth and influence, now lay as broken as their futures. In their eyes, she saw not love or regret, but the smoldering embers of resentment and betrayal.

"My God," Ava thought, her heart racing. "They've destroyed everything – even each other."

The courtroom erupted into a cacophony of whispers and gasps, the air thick with shock and morbid fascination. Ava's eyes darted from face to face, a sea of expressions washing over her like a feverish dream.

"Did you hear? The Summers..." a woman hissed, her pearls gleaming like teeth in the harsh fluorescent light.

"Serves them right," a man growled, satisfaction dripping from his words like venom.

Ava's chest tightened, her breath catching in her throat. The truth of Evelyn and John's actions, laid bare for all to see, hung in the air like a miasma. She caught snippets of conversation, each one a dagger of reality twisting in her gut.

"Security, please escort the defendants out," the judge's voice cut through the din, sharp as a razor.

As if in a trance, Ava found herself swept along in their wake. The courthouse doors loomed before them, a portal to a world that felt both familiar and alien.

The moment they stepped outside, chaos erupted. A sea of reporters surged forward, their questions a relentless barrage.

"Mr. Summers, how does it feel to lose everything?"

"Mrs. Summers, any comments on your husband's infidelity?"

Cameras flashed, each burst of light searing the scene into Ava's retinas. She blinked rapidly, trying to clear the spots from her vision.

"This is madness," she thought, her heart hammering against her ribs.

Beside her, Evelyn's face was a mask of cold fury. "No comment," she spat, her words laced with ice.

John, his composure fracturing, muttered under his breath, "Vultures, the lot of them."

As they were herded towards waiting vehicles, Ava caught a final glimpse of the Summers. In the harsh light of day, stripped of their power and pretense, they looked small, broken. The thought sent a shiver down her spine.

"Is this justice," she wondered, "or just the beginning of a different kind of nightmare?"

Ava stumbled into the quiet sanctuary of her car, her legs trembling beneath her. She gripped the steering wheel, knuckles white, and drew in a shaky breath. The world outside seemed muffled, distant, as if she were viewing it through a veil of gauze.

"It's over," she whispered, the words tasting strange on her tongue. "It's finally over."

Memories flickered through her mind like a twisted slideshow - the accusations, the threats, the sleepless nights. Each one a scar on her psyche, a reminder of the battle she'd fought.

A tap on the window startled her. Her lawyer, concern etched on his face, mouthed, "Are you alright?"

Ava nodded mechanically, not trusting her voice. As he walked away, she caught sight of her reflection in the rearview mirror. The woman staring back at her was a stranger - hollow-eyed, battle-worn, yet somehow... stronger.

"Who are you now?" she asked her reflection, the question hanging in the air like a specter.

Across town, in a stark conference room, the Summers' empire crumbled.

"I want the house," Evelyn hissed, her words dripping with venom.

John's laugh was mirthless, a sound like breaking glass. "You'll get the guest house, nothing more."

Their lawyers exchanged weary glances as the couple tore into each other, their once-united front now a battlefield of bitter recriminations.

"This is what we've become," John thought, watching Evelyn's carefully manicured nails tap a staccato rhythm on the polished table. "Two wolves, tearing at the carcass of our marriage."

The proceedings dragged on, each concession and demand a wound to their pride. As night fell, casting long shadows across the room, John felt a chill creep up his spine. The future loomed before him, vast and empty, a yawning chasm of uncertainty.

"Is this how it ends?" he mused, his voice barely a whisper. "Not with a bang, but with the scratch of a pen on paper?"

Evelyn's eyes met his, a flicker of something - regret? fear? - passing between them. For a moment, they were transported back to happier times, before ambition and revenge had poisoned their hearts.

But the moment passed, quick as a lightning strike, leaving only the acrid taste of ashes in its wake.

Ava's phone buzzed, the screen illuminating her face in the dim light of her living room. She read the message, her brow furrowing.

"The Summers... divorced," she murmured, her voice a mixture of disbelief and something darker.

A chill crept up her spine as she set the phone down, her mind reeling. The satisfaction she'd expected to feel was there, but it was tainted by an unexpected twinge of empathy.

"They were monsters," she whispered to the empty room, "but even monsters can bleed."

She paced, her footsteps echoing in the silence. The walls seemed to close in, memories of the trial pressing against her like phantom hands.

"Is this really the end?" she wondered aloud, her voice trembling.

The clock ticked, each second a reminder of the time she'd lost to their machinations. Yet, as she gazed out the window at the star-studded sky, a spark of hope ignited in her chest.

"It's over," Ava breathed, the words tasting of liberation. "It's finally over."

She closed her eyes, feeling the weight of the past slipping away. When she opened them again, the world seemed brighter, full of possibility.

"A new chapter," she mused, a small smile playing on her lips. "My chapter."

As dawn broke, painting the sky in hues of pink and gold, Ava stood tall, ready to face whatever came next. The shadows of yesterday still lingered, but they no longer held power over her. She was free, at last, to write her own story.

The clink of glasses and murmur of voices filled the small bistro, a stark contrast to the oppressive silence of the courtroom. Ava sat at the center of a table crowded with familiar faces, their eyes shining with admiration and relief.

"To Ava," Sarah, her closest confidante, raised her glass. "The bravest woman I know."

The toast echoed around the table, but Ava's smile didn't quite reach her eyes. She sipped her wine, the bitterness on her tongue a reminder of the ordeal's lingering aftertaste.

"I couldn't have done it without all of you," Ava said softly, her gaze sweeping across the faces of her supporters. "Your faith... it kept me going when I wanted to give up."

A chorus of supportive murmurs rose, but Ava's mind drifted. The Summers' faces flashed before her - Evelyn's defiant sneer, John's crumbling facade. She shuddered imperceptibly.

"Ava?" Tom, a fellow PTA member, touched her arm gently. "You okay?"

She blinked, forcing a wider smile. "Of course. Just... processing, I suppose."

"We understand," Lisa chimed in. "What you've been through... it's a lot."

Ava nodded, grateful for their understanding but feeling suddenly claustrophobic. The walls seemed to close in, the chatter becoming a dull roar in her ears.

"Excuse me," she murmured, rising abruptly. "I need some air."

Outside, the cool night air caressed her flushed cheeks. Ava leaned against the brick wall, her heart pounding. Victory, she realized, tasted bittersweet. The admiration of her peers felt like a heavy cloak, threatening to smother her.

"You don't have to be strong all the time," a voice whispered in her mind. "It's okay to feel... conflicted."

Ava closed her eyes, inhaling deeply. The scent of nearby jasmine mingled with the acrid tang of cigarette smoke, a fitting metaphor for her current state of mind. She was free, yes, but the shadows of her ordeal still clung to her like cobwebs.

"One day at a time," she murmured to herself, straightening her shoulders. "One step forward."

With a final deep breath, Ava turned back to the bistro. Her friends waited inside, their support a balm to her wounded spirit. She would celebrate, yes, but she would also allow herself to heal. The road ahead was long, but for the first time in months, Ava felt ready to walk it.

Chapter 17

The autumn breeze whispered secrets as Ava Jennings stepped from her car, a shiver crawling up her spine. Pine View Elementary loomed before her, its brick facade a familiar specter. She hesitated, hand on the door handle, before steeling herself to enter.

Shadows danced in the hallways as Ava's footsteps echoed. The scent of chalk and disinfectant assaulted her senses, a reminder of routine that did little to quell the unease in her stomach. She couldn't shake the feeling of being watched, even as she nodded to passing students.

The staff room door creaked open, revealing her colleagues huddled around the coffee maker. Ava pasted on a smile, hoping it masked the hollowness she felt inside.

"Morning, everyone," she said, her voice steadier than she felt.

"Ava! How was your weekend?" chirped Sarah, the overly enthusiastic first-grade teacher.

Ava's mind raced, searching for a believable lie. "Oh, quiet. Just some gardening," she replied, avoiding eye contact.

"You always keep that yard so tidy," remarked John, sipping his coffee. "Any exciting plans for the fall?"

The word 'fall' sent a chill through Ava. Images of falling leaves, of bodies falling, flashed unbidden in her mind. She gripped the edge of the counter, willing the memories away.

"Nothing concrete yet," Ava managed, her smile brittle. "How about you all?"

As her colleagues chattered about upcoming holidays and school events, Ava's thoughts drifted. She nodded at appropriate intervals, all the while wondering how long she could maintain this facade. The weight of her secrets pressed down, threatening to suffocate her in this cheerful room.

"Ava?" Sarah's voice cut through her reverie. "You seem distracted. Everything okay?"

Ava blinked, realizing she'd been staring blankly at the wall. "Just a bit tired," she lied smoothly. "Nothing a strong cup of coffee won't fix."

As she poured herself a mug, Ava's hand trembled slightly. She took a deep breath, reminding herself that her mask was necessary. For the children. For the community. For her own survival.

The bell rang, signaling the start of another day. Another performance in this macabre play of normalcy. Ava straightened her shoulders and turned to face her colleagues with a bright smile that never quite reached her eyes.

"Well, duty calls," she said, her tone light but her heart heavy. "Have a wonderful day, everyone."

As Ava left the staff room, she couldn't shake the feeling that her carefully constructed world was slowly unraveling, thread by damning thread.

The fluorescent lights flickered ominously as Ava made her way down the empty corridor, her footsteps echoing in the silence. A chill ran down her spine, though whether from the air conditioning or her own mounting dread, she couldn't be sure.

Principal Davis's office loomed ahead, a portal to another confrontation with her growing unease. She paused, hand hovering over the doorknob, before steeling herself and entering.

"Ah, Ava," Principal Davis greeted, his smile not quite reaching his eyes. "Just the person I wanted to see."

Ava's heart quickened. "Oh?" she replied, striving for nonchalance. "What can I do for you, Principal Davis?"

He gestured to a chair. "Please, sit. We need to discuss the upcoming PTA meeting."

As Ava lowered herself into the seat, she couldn't shake the feeling of being a student called to the principal's office. She clasped her hands tightly in her lap, willing them not to tremble.

"I've been thinking about our fundraising goals," Principal Davis began, his tone deceptively casual. "We need something... different this year. Something to really engage the community."

Ava nodded, her mind racing. "I've been working on some ideas," she offered, her voice steady despite the turmoil within. "Perhaps a charity auction? Or a community talent show?"

Principal Davis leaned forward, his gaze piercing. "Excellent suggestions, Ava. Your dedication to this school is... admirable."

Was that a hint of suspicion in his voice? Ava's pulse quickened. "It's the least I can do," she replied, her smile a brittle mask.

As they continued to discuss logistics, Ava couldn't help but wonder: How much did Principal Davis really know? And how long before her carefully constructed facade crumbled under the weight of her secrets?

The lunchroom buzzed with childish chatter, a discordant symphony that grated on Ava's frayed nerves. She forced a smile, her lips stretched thin over clenched teeth as she approached a table of wide-eyed students.

"Mrs. Jennings!" a girl with pigtails chirped, her innocence a stark contrast to the shadows lurking in Ava's mind. "Will you listen to my poem?"

Ava's heart constricted. "Of course, sweetheart," she murmured, settling onto the bench. The child's words washed over her, a lilting cadence that spoke of sunshine and butterflies. How long ago had her own thoughts been so pure?

A boy tugged at her sleeve, his eyes brimming with unshed tears. "Tommy stole my dessert," he whispered, his voice quavering.

Ava's hand trembled as she patted his shoulder. "Let's see what we can do about that," she soothed, all the while thinking, If only your problems were so simple, child. If only you knew the true monsters that walk among us.

As the lunch period waned, Ava found herself before a vibrant mural adorning the hallway. Splashes of color danced across the wall, a stark contrast to the greyscale world she inhabited.

"Our art therapy program," she explained to a passing teacher, her voice hollow. "A way for the children to express themselves."

But what lies beneath the cheerful façade? she wondered. What darkness do these innocent brushstrokes conceal?

The hallway's fluorescent lights flickered ominously as Ava made her way to the teachers' lounge, each step echoing like a funeral march. She pushed open the door, the creak of hinges sending a shiver down her spine.

Inside, raised voices sliced through the air. Mrs. Thompson and Mr. Reeves stood nose to nose, their faces contorted in anger.

"You can't possibly think canceling the field trip is the right decision!" Mrs. Thompson hissed, her eyes flashing.

Mr. Reeves scoffed, "With the recent budget cuts, we have no choice!"

Ava's heart raced, her pulse a thunderous drumbeat in her ears. She stepped between them, her voice steady despite the tremor in her hands. "Please, let's take a breath. There may be a solution we haven't considered."

As she spoke, Ava's mind whirled. How many more conflicts lurked beneath the school's cheerful veneer? How many more cracks in the foundation threatened to bring it all crashing down?

"What if," she began, her words carefully measured, "we organize a fundraiser? Something to engage the community and raise the necessary funds?"

The tension in the room slowly ebbed, replaced by a cautious optimism. Ava watched as her colleagues nodded, their earlier animosity fading like mist in the morning sun.

"We could plan a carnival," Mrs. Thompson suggested, her anger giving way to excitement.

Mr. Reeves chimed in, "I know some local businesses that might sponsor booths."

As they brainstormed, Ava felt a familiar darkness creeping at the edges of her consciousness. How easily they moved on, unaware of the secrets that haunted these halls. She plastered on a smile, all the while wondering, What nightmares will this carnival bring?

The hallway's fluorescent lights flickered, casting eerie shadows as Ava made her way to her office. A voice, soft as a whisper yet sharp as a knife, cut through the silence.

"Mrs. Jennings?"

Ava turned, her heart skipping a beat. Mrs. Lawson, a parent she'd helped recently, stood there, eyes glistening with unshed tears.

"I... I wanted to thank you," Mrs. Lawson stammered, her voice trembling. "What you did for Tommy, helping him through his... difficulties. It's made all the difference."

Ava's smile was a mask, hiding the storm of emotions beneath. "I'm glad I could help," she replied, her tone warm yet guarded.

As Mrs. Lawson embraced her, Ava's mind raced. If only she knew the true cost of that help, the dark bargains struck in secret corners.

"You're a blessing to this school," Mrs. Lawson said, releasing her.

Ava nodded, guilt gnawing at her insides. "Thank you," she managed, before retreating to her office.

Once inside, she sank into her chair, the weight of her actions pressing down on her. The room seemed to close in, shadows dancing at the edges of her vision.

What have I become? she thought, her breath coming in short gasps. The gratitude, the admiration – it was all built on a foundation of lies and manipulation.

She closed her eyes, remembering the choices that led her here. Each one a step deeper into the abyss, each one justified by the greater good.

A single tear rolled down her cheek as she whispered to the empty room, "At what point does the end stop justifying the means?"

The silence that answered was deafening.

The shadows in Ava's office seemed to pulse with each beat of her heart, a rhythmic reminder of the darkness that now coursed through her veins. She drew a shuddering breath, steeling herself against the onslaught of doubt and regret that threatened to consume her.

"No," she whispered, her voice barely audible in the oppressive silence. "I can't falter now. Not when there's still so much to be done."

Ava rose from her chair, her movements deliberate and controlled. She approached the window, gazing out at the playground where children laughed and played, blissfully unaware of the burdens carried by those who watched over them.

"For them," she murmured, pressing her palm against the cool glass. "It's all for them."

A knock at the door startled her from her reverie. "Mrs. Jennings?" came a tentative voice. "The budget meeting is about to start."

Ava turned, her face a mask of calm composure. "Thank you, Sarah. I'll be right there."

As she gathered her papers, Ava's mind raced with plans and contingencies. The PTA, the fundraisers, the endless meetings – each a piece in a larger puzzle, a puzzle only she could see in its entirety.

"One more day," she told herself, straightening her jacket. "One more day of smiles and nods, of secrets and lies."

Ava strode from her office, her heels clicking a staccato rhythm on the linoleum floor. The hallway stretched before her, a gauntlet of fluorescent lights and cheerful posters that seemed to mock her inner turmoil.

As she pushed open the door to the conference room, Ava's lips curved into a practiced smile. "Good afternoon, everyone," she said, her voice warm and confident. "Shall we begin?"

The meeting passed in a blur of numbers and proposals, but Ava's mind remained sharp, calculating. As the last of the attendees filed out, she lingered, gathering her thoughts for the challenges that lay ahead.

"Another day, another battle," she muttered, her fingers tracing the edge of the table. "But the war is far from over."

With a final glance at the empty room, Ava turned and walked towards the exit, each step carrying her closer to the precipice of her own making. The school's double doors loomed before her, a threshold between two worlds – the façade of normalcy she presented to the world, and the treacherous path she walked in secret.

As she stepped into the fading afternoon light, Ava's resolve hardened. Whatever came next, whatever price she had to pay, she would face it head-on. For the children, for the community, for the greater good that only she could see.

The parking lot stretched before her, a sea of asphalt and metal, each vehicle a silent witness to her departure. Ava's own car waited, a sanctuary and a prison, ready to carry her towards whatever dark destiny awaited.

Chapter 18

The courthouse loomed before Ava, its stone facade weathered by time and secrets. Her footsteps echoed on the marble steps as she ascended, each one bringing her closer to a reckoning long overdue. The weight of injustice pressed upon her shoulders, threatening to crush her resolve. But Ava's jaw was set, her eyes burning with quiet determination as she pushed through the heavy oak doors.

Inside, shadows danced across vaulted ceilings. Ava's heart raced, the pounding in her ears drowning out the hushed whispers that seemed to emanate from the very walls. She wondered, not for the first time, if the ghosts of past judgments lingered here, bearing witness to her plight.

Mr. Thompson appeared at her elbow, his presence both comforting and unsettling. "Are you ready, Ava?" he asked, his voice low and urgent.

She nodded, unable to trust her voice. As they walked towards the courtroom, Ava's mind wandered to Evelyn and John. Were they here already, lying in wait like vipers poised to strike? The thought sent a chill down her spine.

In a secluded corner, Mr. Thompson began to outline their strategy. "We have a strong case," he assured her, his confidence a balm to her frayed nerves. "The evidence is irrefutable."

"But what if-" Ava started, her voice catching.

"No 'what ifs,'" Mr. Thompson interrupted gently. "Justice will be served today. The Summers' reign of terror ends here."

Ava wanted to believe him, but doubt gnawed at her insides. How many times had Evelyn and John slipped through the cracks of justice, their wealth and influence a shield against consequences?

"Remember," Mr. Thompson continued, his eyes boring into hers, "you're not just fighting for yourself. You're fighting for every child, every parent who's ever felt powerless against their machinations."

His words stirred something within Ava - a flicker of hope, perhaps, or the stirring of righteous anger. She straightened her spine, meeting his gaze with renewed determination.

"Let's end this," she said, her voice barely above a whisper but carrying the weight of years of suffering and resilience.

As they turned towards the courtroom doors, Ava couldn't shake the feeling that beyond them lay not just a legal battle, but a reckoning with the very demons that had haunted her for so long. The air grew thick with anticipation, and for a moment, Ava swore she could hear the echoes of past injustices crying out for retribution.

A hush fell over the courtroom as the judge entered, his black robes billowing like storm clouds. Ava's heart stuttered, her palms slick with sweat. The judge's gaze, cold and impassive, swept across the room, settling briefly on Ava before moving on. She shivered involuntarily.

Whispers, like dry leaves skittering across pavement, rustled through the spectators. Ava caught fragments - "...Summers' money..." "...poor woman doesn't stand a chance..." She clenched her jaw, willing herself not to turn around.

Don't let them see your fear, she thought, her nails digging crescents into her palms. *You've come too far to falter now.*

The judge's gavel cracked like thunder, silencing the murmurs. "Court is now in session," he intoned, his voice as dry and unyielding as ancient parchment.

Ava's legs felt leaden as she rose, then sank into the hard wooden chair at the plaintiff's table. Her gaze drifted inexorably across the room, drawn like a moth to flame. There they sat - Evelyn and John Summers, pristine and polished, twin masks of cool disdain.

Evelyn's eyes met hers, and Ava felt a chill race down her spine. In those eyes, she saw not just contempt, but a hunger - a predator's gleam that spoke of battles yet to come. Ava's resolve crystallized, hardening like amber around the fear in her chest.

I see you, Ava thought, her gaze never wavering. *I see the rot beneath your perfect facade. And I will drag it into the light, no matter the cost.*

The air between them crackled with unspoken challenge, a silent declaration of war. As the proceedings began, Ava clung to that moment, steeling herself for the battle ahead.

Mr. Thompson rose, his tall frame casting a long shadow across the courtroom floor. The fluorescent lights flickered overhead, casting an eerie pallor on his face as he approached the jury.

"Ladies and gentlemen," he began, his voice a low, sonorous rumble that seemed to reverberate through Ava's very bones. "We stand here today in the shadow of a grave injustice."

Ava's heart thrummed a staccato beat against her ribs as she watched him, mesmerized. The jury leaned forward, caught in the gravitational pull of his words.

"My client, Ava Jennings, a pillar of this community, has been the victim of a vicious and calculated attack on her character and livelihood." Mr. Thompson's eyes glinted like shards of obsidian as he gestured towards Evelyn and John. "The defendants, driven by spite and malice, orchestrated a campaign of lies that nearly destroyed Ms. Jennings' life."

A cold sweat beaded on Ava's brow. She could feel Evelyn's gaze boring into her, sharp as an ice pick.

Don't look, she told herself. *Don't give her the satisfaction.*

Mr. Thompson's voice dropped to a haunting whisper. "Imagine, if you will, the terror of being falsely accused. The suffocating weight of lies closing in around you, threatening to snuff out everything you've built..."

As he painted a vivid picture of her ordeal, Ava found herself transported back to those dark days. The walls of the courtroom seemed to close in, echoing with the whispers of accusations long past.

Suddenly, a harsh bark of laughter cut through the air like a knife. Evelyn's lawyer, a shark-eyed man with a smile like a crimson gash, stood.

"Your Honor," he sneered, "this melodramatic display is nothing but smoke and mirrors. The real villain in this sordid tale sits before you, masquerading as a victim."

Ava's breath caught in her throat. The lawyer's words slithered through the courtroom, poisonous and insidious.

He's trying to twist everything, she realized, a familiar dread coiling in her gut. *Just like before.*

As the accusations flew, Ava clung to her resolve like a lifeline, even as the shadows of doubt crept ever closer.

Ava's heart pounded as she took the stand, her fingers trembling imperceptibly as she smoothed her sensible skirt. The courtroom's oppressive silence pressed down upon her like a leaden shroud.

"Ms. Jennings," Mr. Thompson began, his voice a gentle lifeline in the suffocating atmosphere, "please tell the court about the events leading up to your arrest."

Ava swallowed hard, her gaze flickering briefly to Evelyn's icy stare before steadying. "It was a Tuesday," she began, her voice low but unwavering. "I was preparing for a PTA meeting when..."

As she recounted the nightmarish sequence of events, Ava felt a curious detachment, as if watching herself from afar. The words poured forth, painting a vivid tableau of betrayal and injustice.

"...and in that moment, as the officers led me away, I saw my entire life crumbling before my eyes," she concluded, a single tear tracing a silvery path down her cheek.

The courtroom hung suspended in a breathless hush.

Evelyn's lawyer rose, a predatory gleam in his eye. "Ms. Jennings," he purred, circling like a shark scenting blood, "isn't it true that you harbored resentment towards my client's son?"

Ava's spine stiffened. *Here it comes,* she thought grimly. *The twist of the knife.*

"No," she replied firmly, meeting his gaze. "I've only ever wanted the best for all the children, including Oliver."

The lawyer's lips curled in a sneer. "And yet, multiple witnesses claim you singled him out for punishment. How do you explain that?"

Ava took a steadying breath, pushing back the rising tide of panic. *Stay calm,* she reminded herself. *The truth is your shield.*

"I treated Oliver exactly as I did every other child," she stated, her voice ringing with quiet conviction. "If he received consequences, it was because of his actions, not any personal vendetta."

As the cross-examination continued, Ava felt herself walking a tightrope over an abyss of doubt and accusation. Yet with each carefully measured response, she wove a tapestry of truth that even the lawyer's sharpest barbs couldn't unravel.

The air in the courtroom thickened, heavy with unspoken truths and barely concealed animosity. Mr. Thompson rose, his face a mask of grim determination. "Your Honor, I call Detective Marcus Johnson to the stand."

A collective intake of breath rippled through the spectators as Detective Johnson strode forward, his piercing blue eyes scanning the room. As he took his seat, Ava felt a flicker of hope ignite in her chest. *This is it,* she thought. *The moment of reckoning.*

"Detective Johnson," Mr. Thompson began, his voice steady, "can you please describe the evidence you uncovered regarding the drug planting conspiracy?"

Johnson leaned forward, his voice a low rumble that seemed to reverberate through the hushed courtroom. "We discovered a series of text messages between Mrs. Summers and an known drug dealer," he stated, his words measured and precise. "These messages detailed the purchase and planned placement of the narcotics in Ms. Jennings' classroom."

Ava's gaze flickered to Evelyn, whose face had drained of all color. John sat rigid beside her, his jaw clenched so tightly Ava could almost hear his teeth grinding.

"Furthermore," Johnson continued, his steely eyes never wavering, "we found traces of the same narcotic substance on Mrs. Summers' personal effects. The chemical signature matched exactly with what was found in Ms. Jennings' classroom."

A low murmur rippled through the courtroom. Ava felt a chill creep up her spine. *How far would they have gone?* she wondered, the true scope of their malice finally dawning on her.

Suddenly, Evelyn's lawyer sprang to his feet. "Objection, Your Honor! This so-called evidence is circumstantial at best!"

The judge's gavel cracked like a gunshot. "Overruled. Continue, Detective."

As Johnson methodically laid out the damning evidence, Ava watched the Summers' carefully constructed facade crumble. Their eyes darted about like trapped animals, the weight of their sins finally catching up to them.

The truth always finds a way, Ava thought, a grim satisfaction settling in her bones. *No matter how deep you try to bury it.*

The courtroom air grew thick with tension as Mr. Thompson called his next witness. Mrs. Thompson, Ava's longtime colleague, approached the stand with quiet dignity. Her soft curls, now streaked with silver, caught the harsh fluorescent light as she settled into the witness box.

"Mrs. Thompson," Mr. Thompson began, his voice gentle but firm, "how long have you known Ms. Jennings?"

"Over a decade now," she replied, her eyes finding Ava's. A ghost of a smile played on her lips. "She's been the heart of Pine View Elementary since the day she arrived."

Ava felt a lump form in her throat. *The heart of Pine View.* How close had she come to losing everything?

As Mrs. Thompson spoke, her words painted a vivid picture of Ava's dedication and kindness. The jury leaned forward, captivated by tales of late nights preparing for school events, of comforting children in distress, of rallying the community during times of need.

"And how did the accusations affect Ms. Jennings?" Mr. Thompson probed.

Mrs. Thompson's voice wavered. "It... it broke her. The light in her eyes dimmed. The children whispered behind her back. Parents who once praised her now crossed the street to avoid her." She paused, her gaze hardening as it fell on Evelyn and John. "They didn't just accuse her. They tried to erase her."

A chill crawled up Ava's spine. *Erased.* That's exactly how it had felt.

As Mrs. Thompson stepped down, Mr. Thompson approached the jury for his closing statement. His eyes blazed with righteous fury.

"Ladies and gentlemen," he began, his voice low and intense, "you've heard the evidence. You've seen the lengths to which the defendants went to destroy an innocent woman's life. All for what? Petty revenge? A misguided sense of entitlement?"

He paced before them, each step punctuating his words. "They planted drugs. They spread lies. They weaponized a community's trust against one of its most devoted members."

Ava's heart raced. She could feel the weight of the jury's gaze upon her.

"I ask you now," Mr. Thompson continued, his voice rising, "to hold Evelyn and John Summers accountable. To show them that their wealth and influence cannot shield them from the consequences of their actions. To prove that in this courtroom, justice still prevails."

As he finished, a heavy silence fell over the room. Ava closed her eyes, exhausted yet hopeful. *Let it be over,* she thought. *Let the truth finally set me free.*

The judge's gavel cracked through the air like a gunshot, shattering the tense silence. Ava's eyes snapped open, her heart a frantic bird in her chest.

"The jury will now retire to deliberate," the judge intoned, his voice as cold and impartial as a tomb. "This court is in recess."

As the jurors filed out, Ava felt the weight of countless eyes upon her. The courtroom buzzed with hushed whispers, a malevolent hive of speculation. She dared not look at Evelyn and John, fearing what she might see in their faces.

What if they win? The thought slithered through her mind, venomous and insidious. *What if, after everything, they still...*

Hours crawled by, each minute an eternity of doubt. Ava paced the halls, her footsteps echoing in the emptiness. When the bailiff finally called them back, she nearly stumbled in her haste.

The jurors entered, their faces unreadable masks. Ava's breath caught in her throat as the foreperson stood.

"Have you reached a verdict?" the judge asked.

"We have, Your Honor."

Ava's world narrowed to a pinpoint, the courtroom fading to a distant blur. She barely registered Mr. Thompson's reassuring hand on her shoulder.

"In the matter of Jennings v. Summers, we find in favor of the plaintiff," the foreperson announced, each word a hammer blow. "We award damages in the amount of five point seven million dollars."

A collective gasp rippled through the courtroom. Ava sat, stunned, as the reality slowly sank in.

It's over, she thought, a hysterical laugh bubbling up in her throat. *It's finally over.*

But as she looked at Evelyn and John's thunderstruck faces, a chill ran down her spine. Something in their eyes told her this was far from the end.

As the judge's gavel struck with finality, a tremor ran through Ava's body. Her face, moments ago etched with worry, now bloomed with an ethereal glow of relief and triumph. The courtroom's oppressive atmosphere dissipated, replaced by a lightness she hadn't felt in months.

"We did it," Mr. Thompson whispered, his voice tinged with awe.

Ava nodded, unable to speak. Her eyes swept the room, taking in the scene that felt both surreal and razor-sharp in its clarity. The judge's stern face had softened slightly, a ghost of a smile playing at the corners of his mouth.

As she rose to leave, Ava's legs trembled. *Is this real?* she wondered, the thought echoing in the caverns of her mind. *Or will I wake to find this all a cruel dream?*

She stepped into the aisle, her movements mechanical. The weight that had burdened her shoulders for so long began to lift, replaced by a dizzying lightness.

"Ava," a familiar voice called. She turned to see Detective Johnson, his usually stoic face creased with a genuine smile. "Congratulations. Justice was served today."

"Thank you," she managed, her voice barely above a whisper. "For everything."

As she neared the courtroom doors, Ava paused. The future stretched before her, no longer clouded by uncertainty and fear. *The children,* she thought, a warmth spreading through her chest. *I can finally focus on them again.*

With a deep breath, she pushed open the heavy doors, stepping out into a world that felt both familiar and utterly transformed.

Don't miss out!

Visit the website below and you can sign up to receive emails whenever Shane Reed publishes a new book. There's no charge and no obligation.

https://books2read.com/r/B-A-LSDAB-EXZDF

BOOKS 2 READ

Connecting independent readers to independent writers.

Did you love *The Vengeful Parent*? Then you should read *Conterfeit Capitalist*[1] by Shane Reed!

[2]

In a sleepy town in Quebec, Tom is a tired businessman ready to escape the grind of his brake pad factory. But when he sells his company, he embarks on a reckless journey that will push the limits of ambition. Armed with nothing but determination, Tom devises an audacious plan to print his own money and become a millionaire overnight.

Meticulously researching the intricacies of the U.S. dollar, Tom's obsession leads him to a clandestine operation where he replicates millions in crisp counterfeit bills. With $250 million in counterfeit twenties at his fingertips, he sets out to sell his ill-gotten gains to a shadowy network of buyers. For years, Tom's scheme goes unnoticed,

---

1. https://books2read.com/u/bzyKPq

2. https://books2read.com/u/bzyKPq

but as greed clouds his judgment, he unwittingly steps into a trap laid by law enforcement.

When a dramatic raid exposes Tom's operation, he faces the terrifying prospect of extradition to the U.S. and a potential 60-year prison sentence. But a clever legal maneuver offers him a lifeline, and after just six weeks behind bars, Tom walks free. Yet, the stakes are higher than ever.

As his trial looms, Tom must decide whether to leverage the remaining $200 million in counterfeit cash as bargaining chips for a lighter sentence. Can Tom outsmart the system one last time?

"Counterfeit Ambitions" is a thrilling tale of greed, ingenuity, and the fine line between success and downfall. Will Tom's audacious gamble lead to freedom, or will it become his ultimate undoing? Discover the electrifying journey of a man who dared to print his own destiny—one bill at a time.

Also by Shane Reed

A Conning Couple Novel
Checkmate
The Great Escape
The Queen's Gambit
The Sicilian Defense
Fool's Mate
The Scottish Game
Stale Mate
The Conning Couple Books 1-5

True Crime
The Sniffing Dog Scam
The Vengeful Parent
Conterfeit Capitalist